GHOST KNIGHTS OF NEW ORLEANS

DAVID ALTHOUSE

Now we unloose a tale formerly of the shadows,
of matters devious, dark, and dreadful.

1

TAKING THE OATH

IN THE CLOSING DAYS OF THE WAR BETWEEN THE STATES, with defeat standing before me, this Southerner considered a decision between love and treasure, and while I opted for both over the one, my plans were interrupted by a great national conspiracy that pulled me toward its center.

'Twas intrigue and treachery on a grand scale, a scheme that threatened to swallow my life, and had the Yankee government ever penetrated its inner workings, a host of men across the country, myself included, would not have lived to recount any story, much less me with the following narrative in hand.

What follows is an account explaining how I joined a certain secret society working toward causes I now see as beyond dubious and how my activities on behalf of the cabal and associations I made within it provided me a ringside seat to one of the greatest conspiracies in the history of the United States.

I stood beside General Stand Watie near Doaksville, Indian Territory on June 23, 1865 as he handed his sword to Federal officers, an act making him the last Confederate general to surrender to Northern forces, some two months after Lee's surrender at Appomattox.

I watched painfully as the bravest man I had ever known gave up the good fight for reasons far outside his control and to men far his lesser. At that moment, I determined to return to New Orleans, the city of my birth, to meet one of the most beautiful ladies in the South, and certainly one of the most cunning, and then collect a treasure cache as rightly mine as anyones. Those thoughts, while pleasant, served as only a partial remedy for the pain of the moment.

You'll trust that I shall divulge the details of the lady, the treasure, and assorted matters of national historical importance in due course.

The war began for me, Drouet Broussard, Confederate scout, spy, and courier, shortly after those peoples comprising what is known as the Five Civilized Tribes of Indian Territory —the Cherokees, Choctaws, Chickasaws, Creeks, and Seminoles—officially allied with the Confederacy in an agreement brokered by noted attorney, writer, Freemason, and Confederate General, Albert Pike.

Albert Pike—remember the name, for the tentacles of him and several others spread far and wide before, during, and after the Great War.

At the war's beginning, each of those tribes severed ties with the United States government and commenced a course with the Confederacy, an honorable, yet albeit mistaken decision when considered in hindsight. After the war, the victorious Yankees chose to use these tribes' allegiance with the South as a reason to strip them of political autonomy and render them dependent upon the government in Washington City for protection and sustenance. I wish Pike had failed in negotiating the alliance. Had he fallen short, we would see those tribes comprising five distinct and fairly autonomous nations in that region of Oklahoma today. While few of us pondered these questions in April of 1861, when the guns of war first boomed, I am forever honored knowing I fought beside such warriors, especially those who fought under my friend, the Indian Swamp Fox, General Watie, a man who showed me the meaning of courage, honor, and tenacity.

General Pike, a close friend of my father who had visited our New Orleans home many times over the years, paid a visit to my family shortly after he secured allegiance from the aforementioned tribes in the Indian Territory. While in New Orleans, he also secured my service as a scout and spy on behalf of those Indian forces. Pike explained that the deal he arranged with the tribes stipulated that the Confederate Government take over all obligations of the United States, that the Confederacy protect against invasions and uprisings in the respective Indian Nations, that the Indians be represented with delegates in the Confederate Congress, that the Indians furnish troops for their own defense, and that they never serve outside Indian Territory. Pike's manner indicated a sense of responsibility on his part for these Indian warriors, and I took his request for my services as a result of that concern.

At the time, I never asked myself why Pike felt compelled to enlist these Indian tribes into Confederate service, but over the years, I ascertained his exact reasons.

Pike knew of my experiences at the Louisiana State Seminary of Learning and Military Academy, an institution where I excelled as a top student under the direction of none other than Major William Tecumseh Sherman. The academy opened in 1860, and I became a beneficiary cadet some months later, receiving instruction there right up until Louisiana seceded on January 26, 1861. Major Sherman resigned as superintendent the following April. During that same time, many of the cadets departed the academy so as to enlist in the Confederate military. I joined the exodus for the same reason. Soon thereafter, Pike queried me about serving as a scout, courier, and spy, roles requiring that I work in close conjunction with the Confederate Indians of Indian Territory.

Pike and Father first met decades earlier through their membership in the Masonic Lodge, an organization enjoying the strong involvement of both men. During the mid-1850s, they commenced a closer friendship with one another and with a cadre of other men who often met at our home to discuss affairs of which I knew nothing about at the time. Their hushed tones behind closed doors indicated the purposes of their meetings were not intended for public awareness. Others in attendance were men such as Judah Benjamin and Senator John Slidell. Both of these men were attorneys by trade who had served as United States Senators from Louisiana. Both went on to serve the Confederacy, Benjamin as Secretary of State and Secretary of the Treasury and Slidell as a foreign diplomat in France. In the years before the war, all maintained a steady stream of communication via mail correspondence and privately-delivered messages. The details of their collective work I shall divulge within these passages in due course.

Pike took an interest in me after Father informed him of reports from the academy in which professors acknowledged in glowing language my abilities in the classroom and in the field. Such talk brings laughter to yours truly, as I am keenly aware that my innate strength is the ability to blend in anywhere and everywhere, no more and no less. Fighting alongside Stand Watie and his Cherokee warriors for nearly four years only served to heighten my abilities to conceal, to elude, and to disappear. If those people from the southeastern woodlands do not know the trick, then it has not been invented. Most importantly, though, fighting alongside Watie honed my greatest strength—the power of knowing who I am and how to be true to

4

myself. The Louisiana State Seminary of Learning and Military Academy did not offer instruction in such matters.

Father held the antiquated belief that privileged Southerners remained exempt from actual military service for the Confederacy, so it was against his wishes that I shook hands with Albert Pike and agreed to perform as a scout and spy among the Indian Nations and fight alongside the warriors of the Five Civilized Tribes.

I stand proud of my service to the Confederacy and to the brave Indian warriors with whom I fought. My work in the field helped secure the capture of the *J.R. Williams*, a Yankee steamboat carrying commissary goods and food for Yankee sympathizers recently returned to the Indian Territory from Kansas and Missouri. Because of information I gleaned from Yankee officers during poker games in Fort Smith during the month of June 1864, Stand Watie and four hundred of his men successfully waylaid the vessel as it rounded Pleasant Bluff near the mouth of the Canadian River while floating from Fort Smith to Fort Gibson. Watie took four hundred Sharps rifles and six hundred new revolvers off of that Yankee boat. To this day, I use a Sharps and wear two revolvers appropriated from that great ambush.

A few months later, in September of 1864, we captured a Yankee supply wagon on its way from Kansas to Fort Gibson to supply Indians loyal to the Federals in the area. We came away with food, clothing, weapons, and other provisions worth well over a million dollars that day, all because of the decisive action of General Watie. Watie always demonstrated certainty and boldness in action, a singular sense of decisiveness that I never forgot.

To be sure, though, I also saw my share of defeat during nearly four years of service. The Battle of Honey Springs comes first to mind as I recall those days. At Honey Springs, for all intents and purposes, the War Between the States in Indian Territory came to a decisive end. The Yankees were emboldened by recent victories at Gettysburg and Vicksburg, and they also feared a Confederate takeover of nearby Fort Gibson, so they determined as necessary a full-scale assault on the Confederates in the area. During the month of July 1863, General Douglas Cooper waited at Honey Springs for General William Cabell and nearly four thousand Southern reinforcements.

Yankee General James Blunt somehow received word of Cabell's imminent arrival on the scene and decided to attack before those reinforcements arrived. To do that, Blunt and his forces endured an all-night trek to the area in and around Honey Springs and commenced engaging Confederates as they came into their view. Blunt's forces enjoyed vastly superior weapons to our Southern fighters on that day. They fought with the best rifles, artillery, and ammunition in the Yankee government's arsenal, while our outnumbered and out-gunned Confederates fought with smoothbore muskets and flintlock shotguns which, because of the morning rain, fired with the most unreliable consistency.

Had Cabell's forces arrived sooner, our Southern forces would have enjoyed a comfortable advantage in men with better weapons and dry powder.

While in Fort Smith in the late afternoon of the previous day, I learned of Blunt's intention of trekking post haste to Honey Springs. I nearly killed two horses attempting to get to Honey Springs before Blunt did. I did not make it in time.

The year before, in March of 1862, I accompanied General Watie at Pea Ridge, Arkansas where we fought under General Benjamin McCulloch. We fought tenaciously even in defeat. We captured Yankee artillery positions and covered the retreat of our Southern forces as Yankees took control.

At Pea Ridge, General Pike led his Indian Brigade of about one thousand soldiers, including a unit of Texas Cavalry. After the battle, when a number of Northern soldiers were found scalped and mutilated on the battlefield, Yankee fingers began pointing in the direction of Pike. The affair led to Pike resigning his commission and, on his way through the door to private life, telling Confederate officials that his Indian troops would never have been at Pea Ridge to begin with had the Confederacy honored its pledge to limit their fighting to battles and skirmishes within Indian Territory.

Many were the days in Indian Territory as we fought against a foe superior in numbers and far better equipped that my thoughts strayed to Father's club, the Pickwick on St. Charles Avenue in New Orleans, and a glass of Sazerac. At the time, I knew the conversations at the Pickwick between Father and his fellow club members often centered around my foolishness in allowing Pike to pull me away from my circle at home and into the wilds of eastern Indian Territory, a land of hard fighting, hard liquor, and hard beds on the ground at night.

After Pea Ridge, Pike made his way south to a secluded and guarded cabin in southwestern Arkansas called Caddo Gap. Once there, he sent me a message through the network that I meet him at once. There, I met with him in the dark of night some several weeks after the defeat at Pea Ridge. The cabin stood guarded by sentries on all sides. From a respectable distance out in the pines, I called out the necessary words to the sentries who immediately barked back permission for me to come ahead.

A sentry opened the front door to the cabin, and I walked through to see once again the bearded, long-haired gentleman who recruited me into Confederate service barely two years prior to that night.

We began a conversation that lasted long into the evening

and into the following morning. Our exchange touched on items I regarded as mere shadows of reality then, but those things are quite tangible now.

Pike advised that I temporarily halt my services on behalf of the forces in the Indian Territory and return to New Orleans straightaway. Pike then showed me the signed paperwork by my superiors allowing this excursion to take place.

"Drouet, New Orleans will not long be free of Yankee tyranny. In a matter of only a few months—if that long—Northern ships shall appear in the gulf and float their way up the Mississippi to a point only mere blocks from our mint on Esplanade Avenue. We need you there when this happens."

"Yankees soon to be in New Orleans? How do you know this?"

"Matters are not always as they appear; a fact of which your own father is too keenly aware. While this Great War engulfs our energies at present, it does not stop a game that has been afoot for many years preceding it."

"Why do you mention the New Orleans mint? Its use as a mint ceased a year ago. The building is now used for housing our Confederate troops stationed in that city."

"There are gold coins, bars, and shavings still in the building that must not fall into Yankee hands. The job falls on you to keep this from happening. The Circle will make use of that gold to advance our purposes after the war, regardless of which side wins. You are to extract the booty out of the mint building and place it where it shall be safe until such time as our society needs it at a future time."

"How do you know there is gold left in the building?"

"Because one of our operatives placed it there in a hidden spot during his employment at the mint."

"You speak of something that involves my father?"

"Yes, a very serious business, and it involves many other

men, some of whom you may remember coming and going at your own home while you were merely a boy."

I vividly remembered numerous meetings over the years at our home attended by my father, Pike, Slidell, Benjamin, George Bickley, the apparent leader of the group, and others. I never asked questions back in those days, but while I stood there before Albert Pike on that dark night in the Ouachita Mountains of southwest Arkansas, my mind certainly raced for answers.

"Drouet, I have kept up with your activities in this war since I first brought you into it. I like how you operate—efficiently, quietly, and without notice. You will be needed after we lose this war, and that is one of the reasons I asked you here tonight."

"Lose the war?"

Pike sat silent and seemingly in deep introspection for several moments before answering.

"I'm afraid we cannot win this war. It has drug on too long now and allowed the government in Washington City to marshal the many forces at its disposal—its industrial might, its many hundreds of thousands of fighting men. Drouet, it is over."

"I cannot believe you say this, general. Just a few weeks ago, you commanded our men on the battlefield as men died all around you, and now you speak nonchalantly of our defeat."

"Just trust me when I say that the cause for which we fight does not die when we are defeated in this war—and defeated we will be."

"You mentioned my father. Is he in some kind of danger? What is going on that I do not know about?"

"All within our Circle are most certainly in danger, even if one of our members speaks of our endeavors."

"What do you need from me?"

"It is the Great Circle, not I, that needs you."

"I will do whatever I need to do in order to help my father."

"We need a courier. One who delivers payments. One who delivers information. One who does what the Circle needs him to do when we need him to do it, and one who works as a shadow as he does it."

"Payments? To whom?"

"To those who have performed services on behalf of the Circle and to those we need to keep quiet. Also, to those who might speak and incriminate our members. But, Drouet, I must tell you that I cannot tell you anything more until you, like your father did many years ago, pledge your loyalty—indeed, your life—to the great Circle of which we have been speaking. And even if you make such a pledge, you will learn our most guarded secrets only over time."

"If my father took this oath of which you speak, then so will I. Let's be on with this business, especially if my father's life is on the line."

Pike then handed me a sheet of paper.

"This is it. Read this to yourself. When you are ready to make your most solemn promise, you will read it aloud."

I read the oath and then, looking to Pike, nodded in the affirmative my intention to make the vow. Pike then went outside and called in the sentinels.

"Drouet, all of these men are members of the Circle who took the same pledge as your father, the same vow you are about to take yourself. Proceed."

"I, Drouet Broussard, do swear to solemnly keep all secrets of the Golden Circle; that I shall faithfully perform whatever I may be commanded, and that I shall always hold myself in readiness to obey the mandates of said Circle whether at bed, or board, at the festive Circle, or at the grave, and if I shall hesitate or divulge the secret, may I incur the severest penalties to which flesh is heir.

"May I be cursed in all the relation of my life, in mind, body, and state, and may the pangs of hell be my eternal portion.

"I feel honored, fellow knights and companions of the Golden Circle, that you have deigned to admit me. No efforts shall be wanting on my part to advance the interests of the organization.

"A distinguished Latin author has justly remarked that it is sweet and profitable to die for one's country. I have but one life and am ready to give it, should it be necessary."

Then Pike and the sentinels uttered in unison, "Whoever dares our cause reveal shall test the strength of knightly steel; and when the torture proves too dull, we'll scrape the brains from out his skull and place a lamp within the shell to light his soul from here to hell."

General Pike then advanced toward me, stopped, and stood facing me at a distance of perhaps two feet. The words he recited from memory ran thus:

"Sir Knight, you have just taken a most solemn adjuration and believe me that you are known to all members in every part of the country. The Knights of the Golden Circle is extensive, and though the government in Washington City is zealous and would freely spend thousands to unveil our designs, all efforts have hitherto been fruitless. No traitor has yet appeared among us, and inevitable ruin awaits the individual who would play the part of Benedict Arnold. No public steps would be taken. He would disappear, and I leave it to you to judge his fate. Dead men tell no tales. Ponder well on these things, and remember, you cannot escape us."

2

KILLING THE KING

BEFORE LEAVING THE SECLUDED CABIN THE FOLLOWING day, Pike allowed for my return to Indian Territory after completing the mission in New Orleans, a move allowing me to see the war through with my Indian comrades, a condition on which I insisted. He also gave me additional names and addresses of key contacts in New Orleans necessary to my mission.

At the time, I wondered why Pike, so soon after the scalping affair at Pea Ridge, still owned enough influence to secure my military leave with the Confederate brass overseeing the war effort in Indian Territory. And obviously, I pondered what connections he might have within the Yankee government in Washington City that he had knowledge of an upcoming Federal invasion of New Orleans.

Eventually, those answers came to me.

I faced a daunting mission in New Orleans. Pike allowed that Yankee warships had been ordered there forthwith and that I take the necessary steps to prevent the treasure hidden within the mint building from falling into Yankee hands when the boats arrived. Interestingly, he seemed to fear the seizure of coin and bars from the mint on Esplanade Avenue far more than he feared the capture of New Orleans itself.

Pike directed me to visit Loreta Janeta Velazquez, one of the top K.G.C. contacts in New Orleans, as soon as I arrived.

In choosing instead to go pay a visit immediately to my father, I disobeyed my first order as an agent of the Knights of the Golden Circle. I longed to see my last remaining parent.

Once home, Marguerite, Father's quadroon mistress, one of the most beautiful ladies in New Orleans, met me at the door. The plaçage system in New Orleans allowed white men and free women of color to form liaisons whereby the man provided for the woman, or placée, and her children for life, even if he had an established white family. Father had loved and idolized Marguerite for as long as I could remember, and, in my eyes, she seemed ever the queen, and that is precisely the rank with which Father treated her. As always, I stood in awe of her appearance and presence, and this meeting was no different. I beheld her raven-black hair, her yellow-tinted, yet somehow cream-colored, skin, and her black-as-night eyes now emanating worry.

Marguerite and I exchanged a few words, and I paid my respects before she motioned me into the next room to Father.

I had been away from home for nearly two years, but Father's face appeared to have aged at least ten. Indeed, his very spirit seemed older. He also appeared afraid, and my father owned a countenance on which I had never before detected a shred of fear.

In the course of our conversation, I informed Father of my newfound membership in the K.G.C. That Father found this news disappointing showed clearly upon his face.

"Are you not happy with this, Father?"

"Did Pike enlist you?"

"Yes. But what is the matter? Is Pike not your friend? He has been many times in this home. He recruited me into the war from the beginning. Right or wrong, I've looked up to him."

"I joined the Circle at the very beginning, over five years ago, and I wish I hadn't."

"Are you not on the best of terms with the most influential of its leaders?"

"I thought I was."

"Something is wrong, Father. What is it?"

"The Circle is not what I thought it was."

"Does it not stand for Southern independence, for the rights of we Southrons to determine our own affairs?"

"I once believed that. There's more to it, Drouet."

I stood silent and confused in front of Father, trying as best I could to make sense of his words—and of his fear.

"You know, neither you nor I possess the qualifications for membership in the Circle, Drouet."

"You entertained its top men in this home on many occasions. Surely what you say is incorrect."

"Have I ever owned slaves?"

"No, Father, you have not. But what does that have to do with anything? You are a businessman, not a man of the plantation. You've never had need of slaves."

"But ownership of slaves is a prerequisite for membership, Drouet."

"Then how were you allowed to join?"

"They allowed me to join under the highest suspicions, and they have never trusted me completely since I took the oath."

"I do not understand. Enlighten me. What does owning slaves have to do with it?"

"It has everything to do with the K.G.C. The original purpose of the Circle was to work toward a 'Golden Circle' of slave-holding territories throughout the Caribbean, Central

America, Mexico, and the present-day states of the Confederate States of America, including the Indian Territory, where you have been lately engaged, with all of this led by Maximilian of Mexico."

"This is unbelievable! The K.G.C. purports to defend the Confederacy at all costs, but you say the grand design is that we bow to Maximilian?"

"Pike, Slidell, Benjamin, and the rest, all under the leadership of Bickley, are the grandest of conspirators, and I was too slow in realizing their true objectives."

"Do they also resent you having Marguerite?"

"Of that, I am not sure. Maybe."

Father's words explained why Pike had been so willing to organize the Five Civilized Tribes of eastern Indian Territory on behalf of the Confederacy. Many within those tribes owned slaves and how better to bring the region into the great Circle than to first engage its people into the fight for Southern secession, a move that, if successful, would count as an important first step in establishing the Circle's ultimate goal—the 'Golden Circle' of slave-holding territories as Father explained.

"Father, Pike somehow knows that New Orleans will be attacked any day now. How does he know this?"

"He knows because he receives secret coded dispatches from K.G.C. members in the Yankee Government."

"From whom?"

"Does the name Andrew Johnson mean anything to you, son?"

"Lincoln's vice president?"

"Yes, but if you value your life, then pretend you are unaware of these facts. Let me lay the facts before you, Drouet. If Pike knows New Orleans will be attacked soon, it is because his Yankee K.G.C. puppets have told him so. And Pike also knows that if New Orleans is successfully taken—which it most surely will be at the hands of a vastly superior Yankee navy—then the life of our beloved Confederacy comes to an end soon."

"Then the life of the K.G.C. also comes to an end, right? Lincoln and the Abolitionists will free the South's slaves, and how does that further the Golden Circle of slave-holding territories?"

"To Pike, Slidell, and Benjamin, the fall of the Confederacy is a mere roadblock. They have plans in place for when our Confederacy crumbles. They have plans in place that were formulated in this very house with my knowledge."

"What plans?"

"They will work to cause as much disruption in the Yankee government as possible toward the end. They will attempt to take the war to Texas and to your Indian Nations with whatever is left of our Confederate forces."

Father's face seemed to have taken on age in the telling of all this. We heard the distant sound of a steamboat horn from the river and Father gazed introspectively through a window.

"Son, I want you to forget about all the K.G.C. men you saw in this house so many years ago. From those men came the 'Kill the King' directive to be carried out at the end, and you should be as far away from civilization as possible when that happens. I wish I could flee too, but alas, I am an old man and shall likely face the consequences."

"Kill the King?"

Father's answer explained the sound of fear in his words and the look of it upon his face.

"Yes, the assassination of Abraham Lincoln."

3

PLANNING MY FIRST ASSIGNMENT FOR THE K.G.C

Before leaving Father, I asked him if I should leave the ranks of the K.G.C.

He responded that no one leaves the K.G.C.

"Just slither within its ranks as unnoticed as possible, play the game, play it smart, wait it out until the end, and, when the end comes, as it most certainly will come, have yourself situated on the other side of the world if possible."

This I determined to do.

I then bathed, shaved and fitted myself out in attire more appropriate for the streets of home. From my old closet, I retrieved numerous items of clothing, including my long cape, an article that allowed for easy concealment of weapons beneath.

From there, I made haste to 57 St. Charles Avenue, home of the Pickwick Club, a members-only affair into which I entered after a long absence. There, I ordered a Sazerac, a drink I had not enjoyed for well over a year, but had tasted in my mind a million times during that period. Father always said a man has to sometimes indulge a bad habit and to never trust a man who doesn't. That night, I indulged my fixation several times before leaving 57 St. Charles. As I reflected on my reason for returning to the Crescent City, though, it suddenly dawned on me that all good things must come to an end. I knew I must get on to business.

Without difficulty, I found the Velazquez residence on Prytania Street, not too many blocks distant from my father's residence.

I knocked on the door to the Velazquez home, and a Confederate officer answered and welcomed me inside even before I had a chance to announce myself. The officer donned a handsome, well-kept uniform with lieutenant insignia on the coat sleeves, a thick mustache swirled on both ends, and a goatee.

"Drouet Broussard, I presume? We have been expecting you. Please take a seat here in the foyer. I will wait with you as Miss Velazquez makes herself ready."

The officer took hold of a small brass hand bell, rang it briskly to notify the lady of the house of her guest, and then he seated himself in a chair on the wall opposite me in the grand foyer. He did not seem like one for small talk, and I offered no opportunities for such engagement. We sat silently for what seemed like an eternity with the tick-tock of a nearby wall clock offering the only reminder that life proceeded apace. Five minutes elapsed. Then ten. Then fifteen. Hearing no other sound from anywhere else throughout the domicile, I soon began to wonder if the lieutenant and myself were actually alone in the place.

Just as I noticed my mind growing more agitated while attempting to resolve the truth of the circumstance, the lieutenant arose, walked to a position maybe three feet from my person, removed the mustache and goatee, and threw off the

Confederate cap which allowed long, flowing, raven-black hair to fall down the back and over the shoulders. The truth of the matter now revealed itself in stunning feminine beauty, and I stood mesmerized while trying to refrain from showing anything other than a stoic poker face. The lithe and lovely lady, a stoic male Confederate lieutenant only seconds before, then removed everything else down to the minimum essentials, and the result certainly deserved my compliments.

"My lady, what I see standing before me could stop a charge of the Mamelukes of the Imperial Guard and easily sink a fleet of Yankee warships out on the river."

"I see that you and I will get along famously. And, yes, if I have to use what you see standing before you to complete this mission, I will gladly do so."

"Do you often play dress up?"

"I've perfected the art of the disguise, and it serves me well in my current occupation."

"I see this is going to be fun."

"Promise?"

"I'm already finding our collaboration rather enjoyable. And you?"

"We have work to do."

"Oh, yes, that. There's gold hidden inside the mint, and we have to get it out. How could I forget?"

"I hope you have constructive ideas."

"I do. Several glasses of Sazerac at the Pickwick helped ignite my imagination, and my mind formulates ideas as we speak."

"And?"

"I know how and when—when to the day."

"My interest is piqued. Please go on."

"Do we know where inside the mint building the gold is located?"

"We do. It is stashed behind a false wall of a closet at the rear of the building on the first floor, nearest the streets of Decatur and Barracks."

"And how did the gold end up there?"

"Our operative worked in the mint and, over time, as opportunities arose, managed to build quite a nice collection of bars, dust, and shavings behind the false wall."

"What do you mean by shavings?"

"Before a coin is struck, someone is responsible for making sure it meets the uniform weight and size requirement. If a blank coin weighs too much or is too large, someone is responsible for shaving it down to the uniform weight and size."

"Are not these shavings collected to make additional coins?"

"You are right. Nothing is wasted when it comes to gold."

"So, how did the shavings make it from the floor to the closet?"

"During the heat of summer, workers oftentimes convinced their employer to open the windows to allow in fresh air. Sometimes the mint staff allowed the windows open, sometimes not. It depended on their mood. Anyway, on windy days the shavings on the floor could be blown this way and that inside the building and become lost in the accounting efforts. Our operative used this weakness in the system to amass a sizeable amount of shavings."

"Pray, how did our operative manage to secure gold bars and ingots and whisk said material into this closet?"

"The bars were kept in a vault. The door of the vault was constructed of metal bars through which one could see the contents within. At the bottom of the door, on the door handle side, the door could be pried apart wide enough to allow our operative, using a long metal prod thinner in size than a cigarette, hooked at the end, to dislodge the bars from the stacks and drop them to the floor. The metal prod was then used to nudge the bars to the door where he pulled them through. He then hurried the bars quickly to the closet where he hid them behind the false wall. When our operative walked out the door to go home at the end of the day, there wasn't a spec of gold to be found on his body."

"Our operative is a good thief. He wasn't really stealing in the strictest sense. He was relocating."

"Correct. We shall be the ones stealing it—if we can."

"We can. Although, I must say it feels strange thinking about stealing from the Confederacy, a government for which I have fought with all my heart for over a year."

"This is a K.G.C. job. Pike, Benjamin, and Slidell believe The Circle was fighting for the Confederacy before there was a Confederacy. So, what ideas have you?"

"We make our move as soon as we hear the booms from the Yankee warships when they attack. That could happen any day now, and it could happen at any time during the day or night. We must be ready when that time comes. One other thing...the mint building was not built to be a military fortification. As soon as the guns of the Yankee warships blast from the river every soldier in the mint building will depart the premises. From a military standpoint, the mint building is a place to flee —not defend—when the attack commences. The troops will exit the building post-haste and immediately take up positions along the river to fire on the enemy boats. There should be nary a man in the mint building even ten minutes after the shooting starts. Anyone left behind on Esplanade Avenue will likely be sick or injured soldiers or civilians."

"So, we simply walk in, extract the gold and nonchalantly make our way through the Vieux Carre and away?"

"No, *I* simply walk in, extract the gold and then we

nonchalantly make our way through the Vieux Carre and away."

"Where will I be in all of this?"

"You, my master of disguise, shall be in costume. You will wait in the wagon while I make the necessary trips in and out of the building to remove the gold. It is imperative that you stay in the wagon until the operation is fully completed."

"How will I be dressed?"

"More about that later. Oh, and one other thing. You and I must be inseparable until the operation is complete."

"I thought there might be some kind of catch."

"No catch. As soon as we hear the first sign of attack, we will not have time to find each other, get you into costume and begin. No, at the first sign of attack, we move with lightning speed. We get you into costume at once. And I mean fast. Then, we board our wagon and make a dash to the mint. We have to make our move in the mint after our Confederate forces leave the premises and before the Yankees decide to camp out there themselves after they take the city."

"Once retrieved from behind the false wall of the closet, to where are we transporting the contents?"

"To a place where only ghosts dare search for it."

"Oh, so it's going to be like that?"

"You will know of the new hiding spot on the night of the attack, and not a day sooner."

"We are currently many blocks from the mint building. Might we find quarters closer to Esplanade Avenue?"

"Yes, my father owns an apartment near Royal and Toulouse, maybe eight blocks distant. We prepare our wagon at once, we attain the items necessary for your disguise if you do not already possess them, and we stay by each other's side beginning now until at least the goal has been successfully achieved."

"At least?"

"At least. And tomorrow we move into comfortable, and might I say lavish, quarters on Royal Street."

"What about tonight?"

"Tonight, I stay here. With you."

4

ROBBING THE CONFEDERATE MINT

Early the following day, Miss Velazquez and I began making important preparations for the business at hand. We secured all the items necessary for her disguise, we appropriated a wagon on which to transport the gold, and we moved more than enough items from her house on Prytania Street to Father's apartment in the Vieux Carre to accommodate her for at least the next two months.

On that same day, we stopped at Father's where I retrieved more clothing from my old rooms.

I wore the aforementioned cape. Underneath, I sported two Colt Model 1855 Sidehammers—single-action affairs, yes, but more than ample firepower at the time for most scrapes. In each of the deep outer pockets of the cape, I carried a razor-sharp blade, Bowies both.

We made our way to the apartment and there we remained for the next several weeks. Velazquez and I rarely left each other's sight, night or day. We made good use of the closeness, oftentimes rehearsing for the important day ahead and going over likely scenarios that might unfold as we attempted the heist. One night we walked to the mint building, and she showed me the layout of the place, which door to enter and the direction to turn inside the building to find the closet.

Then, during the pre-dawn hours of late April 1862, a Saturday, if memory serves, after a long night of little sleep and more than one glass of Sazerac for each of us, the faint crack of cannon fire miles away on the Mississippi interrupted our bliss. Yankee warships full of troops now moved upriver in our direction. I peered outside to the streets of the Vieux Carre and beheld throngs of people in a scene of growing restlessness and chaos. The streets below us were usually quiet at such an hour, but now we had a full-fledged Yankee invasion underway.

At once, Velazquez began getting into character, applying costume, make-up and all the trimmings. I departed to the nearby holding spot for our wagon, harnessed the jack, and then drove the contraption to the alley behind the apartment where I retrieved my partner in crime, now in the full glory of her rather ghastly, but oh, so beautiful and well-applied, get-up.

As we slowly started along our way to Esplanade Avenue, a great thunderstorm blew in to accompany the invading Yankees. In a now wildly chaotic world of booming thunder mixed with the increasing fire of both Confederate and Yankee artillery, lightning flashed and cracked sharply while torrents of rain fell upon us. Instead of cursing the weather, I welcomed it. The more general confusion all around, the better. Luckily, Velazquez lay under a sheet of canvas in the back of the wagon – impervious to the falling rain, but more than aware of the growing turmoil descending upon the city.

Many times along the way we encountered our Confederate troops frantically running to spots along the river from which to fire upon the enemy boats and the Yankee soldiers soon to pour from them. I saw this as good news. The more of our boys making a stand in the city then the fewer of them holed up in the mint building to get in our way.

I pulled the wagon to the rear of the mint building nearest Decatur Street. I, Velazquez, and the jack remained quiet for a few moments as I tried to ascertain the number of men still in the vicinity and within the building. I saw no sign of humanity within from my perch on the wagon, but I wanted a better look. I decided to walk around to the front of the building and peer inside from there. Amidst all the pandemonium, I doubted anyone would notice or care. I reached the front and made my way to the center door underneath the columns. Looking in, I quickly fathomed nothing at all occurring inside and not a solitary soul in my range of vision or within earshot.

That is all I needed to know to confidently commence the job at hand. I returned to the rear of the building and pulled the wagon closer to the rear outer door. The less distance from the wagon to the closet the better, and I knew that many trips back and forth between the two points lay ahead of me, so I got to work.

At the top of a false wagon bottom lay Velazquez covered first with hay and then with the canvas tarp.

"Loreta, I'm going in. Be perfectly still and quiet."

"Just hurry."

I reached the outer door only to find it slightly ajar as if someone—probably a Confederate soldier—had quickly departed the premises and, in haste, failed to close it. Crossing the threshold of the doorway, I committed myself to the task at hand. I cut a quick left and found the closet just a short walk down a hallway.

Inside the closet, I found the typical contents of brooms and mops and assorted tools required for building maintenance. Quickly, I stepped to the back wall of the closet and knocked gingerly up one side of it and down the other. The wall consisted of thin wood strips covered with wallpaper. I kicked it through. Once on the back side of the wall, I saw hinges to one side allowing for an easier, swivel-like opening—a fact unknown to me beforehand. The ingots, bars and tied-off bags that lay all around me, once loaded, nearly filled the area under the wagon's false bottom. The odds of a devastating interruption to the heist greatly increased with the passing minutes, so I made quick work of it, carrying as much as possible on each trip while pretending to casually ignore the increasing state of chaos and anarchy all around us in the Vieux Carre.

Having loaded the last of the contents under the false bottom, I raised the tailboard, hitched it, and climbed aboard. We proceeded along Decatur Street toward Canal Street, first past Ursulines, then St. Philip, then Dumaine, then Jackson Square.

By this time, in order to keep the Yankees from capturing valuable supplies and assets, our Confederates had started setting fire to warehouses, bales of cotton, ships, and docks throughout the city. Great fires went up all around, and smoke blocked what little sunlight that had previously emerged through the rain clouds.

Lines of our citizenry lined the river and shouted curses to the sailors aboard the ships. The Yankee sailors taunted back by simply patting their cannons and smiling. This infuriated the crowd even more, and it also enraged me, try as I might to conceal said fact. I had fought Yankees up in the Indian Nations for over a year, so the invaders in our midst this day were certainly no friends of mine.

Two blocks past Jackson Square, a group of blue-coats, fresh up from the wharves along the river, hailed our merry band to a halt. An officer sporting a sergeant's chevron stood directly in our path and bellowed his rude introduction.

"Halt at once!"

I immediately pulled the wagon to a stop.

"Good morning, Sergeant."

The sergeant began circling and closely inspecting the wagon while his handful of perhaps six men watched on.

"What's your name, rebel?"

"The name is Broussard. Drouet Broussard."

"You look sort of nervous, rebel. Why?"

"Well, my city is under attack by Yankees. I plead guilty to being just a little distraught."

"I guess that makes sense. You would be distraught, wouldn't you?"

"Look around. I'm not the only one."

"Yes, but you look even different from all the rest."

"I should say it has been a rough week for me and my family, to be sure, Sergeant."

"Rough? How so?"

"Well, it's something of a private family matter."

The sergeant walked up to the wagon and placed his hand upon the wet canvas tarp.

"Let's have a look at what you're hauling."

"Sergeant, that is not the best idea. Certainly not a safe idea for you and your men."

"Alright, Broussard. Then you step down here and peel back this canvas and show me what you have under there."

"Sergeant, sir..."

"Now, rebel!"

I stepped down from atop the wagon and pulled the canvas away to reveal the hay.

"What's beneath that hay?"

"What's beneath the hay is covered for good reason, but you are welcome to see."

I began to slowly pull back the hay to reveal a yellow-skinned, blue-splotched version of Loreta Janeta Velazquez.

28

I left a scattering of hay over her face to serve as camouflage.

"You and your men may want to cover your faces and hold your breath, Sergeant."

"What in hell is that?"

"That is my sister, sir."

"Why is she yellow and what are those blue spots?"

"The Fever. She is jaundiced, and those blue marks are internal bleeding."

"The fever?"

"Yellow fever. My sister is dead, sir."

"Is it catchy?"

"It is. But your Yankee guns are helping. So is all of the burning tar hereabouts."

"How's that?"

"The cannon fire and smoke from the tar disrupts the miasma in the air."

"Cover her up at once and get the hell out of here!"

The sergeant and his men stepped aside and made way for our departure, and I wasted no time continuing the journey, exhaling with relief as our wagon lurched forward.

Once out of immediate earshot of anyone, I inquired as to Loreta's condition underneath the tarp and hay, and she wasted no time responding.

"Do as the Yankee said and get us out of here. No talk!"

The jack pulled us along Decatur Street uninterrupted past Canal Street. We turned right on Poydras then eventually took a left on St. Charles. I felt considerably safer the further along we traveled, as our distance from the river and the Yankee boats spewing forth soldiers increased as we drew closer to the Prytania Street residence of my partner in crime.

We arrived at her residence and immediately pulled the wagon through the door of an enclosed wagon house adjacent the home. We pulled the door shut and locked it before making our way inside the Velazquez domicile.

Velazquez removed her makeup and garb in Teutonic time, and I mixed myself a Sazerac even faster.

"There is certainly more entertainment to be had watching you remove that appalling attire than there ever was viewing its application."

"We just pulled off one of the greatest robberies in history, and you think of that? Incorrigible."

"Well, I have to admit I thought of something else as we made our way across town with the booty."

"Pray, enlighten me."

"I'm a Confederate scout and spy who has worked to assist our fighting men in the Indian Territory. I've seen untold horrors fighting on behalf of a cause for which the men inhabiting the mint building fight this very minute. And I used all of this commotion with its fighting and screaming and gunfire as cover to steal treasure belonging to the Confederacy. I have turned against my own."

"There are a few items we need to discuss, Drouet."

"Like what?"

"First of all, the contents of the wagon do not technically belong to the Confederacy. The K.G.C. operative who hid away that loot inside the building did so when the mint belonged to the government of the United States before the war started."

"Why didn't you tell me that days ago?"

"Pike and his associates, most likely directed by George Bickley, wanted to test your allegiance to The Circle. You did well by their estimation; I'm sure."

"What other secrets have you?"

"The only other information to impart is that you must hide

the wagon's contents immediately. You must hide the loot tonight, and you must not tell me where."

"Why can I not tell you?"

"Those are the orders."

"I've already considered the matter. The trickery of concealing the gold will be the final act of our ruse."

"Good. If you do as well in the hiding of it as you did in stealing it, then no one will ever find it."

"I will conceal it where only angels and demons dare tread. Hopefully, the angels will use their influence on my behalf."

5

HIDING THE CACHE

VELAZQUEZ AND I REMAINED INSIDE HER RESIDENCE until the sun went down and while the gloom of Yankee occupation enveloped New Orleans. Mobs comprised of the local citizenry roamed the streets in defiance, but Confederate General Mansfield Lovell surveyed his scant force and realized at once the futility of meaningful resistance. The General told Mayor John Monroe that the Yankees, if faced with spirited defense, would inflict severe damage and casualties upon the city.

The Yankees now controlled New Orleans, the gateway to the lower Mississippi, and the Confederacy now faced imminent doom. I chose to shove such facts from my mind and concentrate instead on matters more pressing to me personally.

I figured since we removed the cache from the mint building in broad daylight in front of seemingly the entire citizenry of New Orleans and an invading Yankee army that I'd get to work concealing it in the same fashion—that is, in plain sight of the entire world.

New Orleans seemed covered in a blanket of death and

destruction. The gold from the mint building would take up residence in a place of similar energy.

When the sun dropped, and full darkness set in, I stepped out to the wagon house, checked the jack, the wagon, and contents, opened the wide door and drove the contraption to a spot located barely one city block distant—to the City of the Dead, also known as Lafayette Cemetery. There, Father owned one of the many above-ground vaults making up this village of ghosts. The family vault of which I mention, originally erected for an uncle who met his end in Europe, but whose body never made it back to New Orleans, had stood empty these many years with uncle's name chiseled on the front. Few knew the crypt stood empty of the body for which it had been constructed to safe keep.

After a long day of thunder and lightning and rain, a thick mist covered the city. The fog slithered along every street and alleyway, as well as through the pathways of the necropolis before me. Along the way, I thought I saw shadow people from the corner of my eyes. I detected them through the darkness and fog. They often showed themselves to me at night, and each time I saw one lurking it immediately transformed from a well-defined dark outline to something akin to a faint puff of dark smoke and then to nothing at all. Marie Laveau, a good friend of my late mother, taught me about these dark phantoms during my youth. She did not claim to know if they are ghosts of the departed or sinister forces from the dark realm. She believed they occasionally acted as omens or portents of something bad yet to happen and that they often reappeared to those in whom they are intensely interested. She never expressed fear when discussing them.

The jack pulled us through the gate and in a matter of about two minutes we arrived at the tomb. I had visited the vault many times as a child and knew that three square stones at the rear base were loose enough to remove, and this feat I accomplished in a short time. Stones now extracted, a crawl space, albeit tight, presented itself allowing me to place my cargo within. I went to work and arranged the bags and bricks inside the crypt as best I could in complete darkness of night and cover of fog, with the shadow people most certainly watching on in silence. Only a crescent sliver of waning moon appeared through the clouds and vapor, a fact making the night's work difficult. I consoled myself with the knowledge that the same darkness and mist also concealed my journey to this city of crypts as well as my movements within.

After appropriating enough gold coins to fill my pockets, I slid out of the chamber and re-inserted the stones in place. From the nearby pathway, I gathered handfuls of dirt which I threw over the wet backside of the tomb to create an undisturbed appearance.

The time to leave lay upon me. The jack and I departed under the cloak of darkness and fog and the watch of the shadow people. Perhaps the gray night men showed themselves because of interest in my nefarious activities of late, maybe because of an upcoming evil.

Maybe both.

6

EVIL AT HAND

No sooner had the Yankees arrived in New Orleans than the time for my departure of the city presented itself.

I had told General Pike I intended to return to my duties in the Indian Nations upon completion of my mission and he had consented.

Before leaving, though, I intended to spend time with my partner in crime, with Father, and with multiple glasses of Sazerac at the Pickwick Club. I plead guilty to enjoying New Orleans for about two weeks longer than necessary and, in hindsight, I am glad I did, for those days after the heist proved the last of Father's life.

I found his lifeless body sitting in his study with a dropped glass nearby, the floor still wet with bourbon. While certainly a man in elder years, Father had appeared relatively vigorous during those days and I stood perplexed at his sudden passing. I stooped to the floor to sniff the remnants of his last drink and detected a garlic-like scent. I strongly suspected he had been poisoned.

I made all arrangements for a funeral service and for placement of his remains in the family tomb. Out of concern for her life, I instructed Marguerite to stay away from Father's home until I returned from Indian Territory. I made arrangements for her to stay with a distant cousin not too many blocks away. Marguerite and I discussed at length how she should remain discreetly out of sight.

The night before leaving for the Indian Nations, I spent a few hours at the Pickwick enjoying first one Sazerac and then another. While feeling the full effects of the drink, I detected queer behavior from surrounding club members—men conversing in hushed tones while seeming to occasionally glance my way, and club staff looking at me with strange expressions. Everyone around me seemed privy to something concerning me of which I remained unaware, and I did not enjoy the feeling. Did they know about the heist? Did they know about Velazquez? Did they know where I stashed the booty?

The elite of New Orleans frequented the Pickwick Club, and I surely knew that some of that same cadre helped create and organize the Knights of the Golden Circle some seven years earlier under the leadership of George Bickley. Some within my midst that night seemed aware of my past transgressions and of foreshadows of things to come. Not enjoying the ambiance, I decided to leave the premises and set out for the Indian Nations the following morning.

I departed 57 St. Charles Avenue and made for Canal Street, crossed it, and then took an alleyway on my way to the apartment deeper in the Vieux Carre. At the opposite end of the dark, narrow thoroughfare stood two dark figures in the shadows, and these were certainly not shadow people. I pondered reversing course to avoid the two but decided to advance and face what was probably the sort of inebriated loiterers I had encountered many times before.

As I advanced to within nearly fifty feet, the two crept from their partly concealed positions and stood directly in my pathway. Without hesitating, I walked straight toward them.

It became obvious the two stood in wait for me, and my thoughts envisioned a probable robbery in my immediate future—that or questioning by Yankees as to the purpose of my late-night prowling.

My heart beat ever rapidly as the distance between me and the alley cats decreased, and so loud was the booms that they rang in my ears. Fear coupled with a genuine interest in their intentions served to heighten the exhilaration of the moment.

As I wedged my way between the two, the one on my left shoved me hard against a brick wall and laughed. The one on my right remained quiet.

"It's time for answers, Broussard."

"Get your damned hands off me before I kill you both."

"Full of swagger, are you? I guess it takes such to pull off what you have."

I charged from my position against the brick wall to attempt a break, but to no avail. The two closed in and commenced a short beating.

"Now, listen very carefully. You are going to tell us where you stashed the plunder, and you are going to tell us right now."

The two stood directly against either side of me, and I knew I couldn't break free from the predicament.

The quiet one finally spoke, but not before a swift and deep punch to my solar plexus.

"Unless you want to die in this alley tonight, you'd best start talking. And those are orders from the top."

I remained quiet and the two, in unison, slammed me against the brick wall again.

Up to then, I had fairly left both hands in the pockets of my cape gripping the handles of my blades. My alleyway enemies made it clear they fancied fights of the eye-to-eye variety, and that proved their undoing. My gut and both sides of my head ached from the blows, and I increasingly grew tired of the stench of their breaths so close to my face. To boot, I received a premonition that maybe these two, or K.G.C. operatives like them, were responsible for poisoning Father.

I had taken about all I intended from the sons of bitches.

The time lay upon me.

I presented both blades in one swift motion, starting deep at the navel of both men and working upward, a stem-to-stern type affair. Even in the darkness, I beheld the whites of eyes now enlarged with shock and figured it a perfect time to finish the job, twisting and ramming both blades deep in my respective victims until the act of their falling separated them from my Bowies.

The two then comprised what looked like a single crumpled heap in the alleyway and I jumped over it as I exited the scene. From there to the apartment, I made sure to avoid any other living human being whether Southern or Yankee, and the latter variety seemed to be increasing in numbers with each passing day.

From then on, especially while in New Orleans, I had to behave as the followed man I probably was, followed by those either paid by K.G.C. leaders to beat out of me the whereabouts of the hidden stash or by those who simply learned of the robbery on their own and wanted to know the location of the booty.

On the following day, during a visit with Velazquez to inform her of my return to the Indian Nations, she notified me of her own imminent departure of the city to partake in yet another mission. I did not ask for details and knew she would not divulge had I done so. In my eyes, she stood as the quintessential loyal K.G.C. agent. I, on the other hand, owned just enough allegiance to The Circle to heed Father's words:

"Just slither within its ranks as unnoticed as possible, play the game, play it smart, wait it out until the end, and, when the end comes, as it most certainly will come, have yourself situated on the other side of the world, if possible."

That did not, however, keep Velazquez and me from enjoying several glasses of Sazerac to complement a more than memorable last rendezvous in New Orleans.

We ended our revelry with me slightly inebriated, but lucid and robust enough to endeavor an escape of my home town, a city now occupied by hordes of Yankees. I also stood coherent enough to understand the irony of attempting a break from a city where killers of Yankee occupiers are shot or hung, all to make a break for the Indian Nations where killers of Yankees are awarded medals. While I love my Crescent City, the thought of returning to a land where Yankees are still fair game seemed gratifying to me.

Loreta and I walked to the front door arm-in-arm. As we kissed goodbye, I felt reluctant to release her from my embrace.

Loreta stood at her front door looking slightly forlorn as I walked toward the street and away.

"Drouet, we will meet again?"

"Just you make sure to finish your duties safely and get back here to me. A bullet has not been made that will keep me from getting back here to you."

Not knowing whose watchful gaze we were under, I bowed slightly and tipped my hat to her. As I turned to close the gate, I glanced again at her and quickly brought my hand to my heart and patted it twice, discreetly inferring my affections for her.

She smiled gently in return and raised her hand to her own heart.

I stepped away as she quickly turned to go back inside her home.

7

WORKING OUTSIDE OF NEW ORLEANS

IN LEAVING NEW ORLEANS, I CHOSE CIRCUITOUS ROUTES.

I journeyed along hidden pathways under the darkness of night while retrieving from memory the location of nearly-forgotten trails discovered during my early years, the sort of thoroughfares known only to the young and carefree. I began to breathe easier as I trekked north and west, putting greater distance between myself and the new Yankee residents of New Orleans. It also felt pleasing to know I left behind scores of K.G.C. thugs who crept amidst the cracks, crevices, and alley-ways of the Crescent City.

To hell with them all. The job of retracing my original tracks back to Caddo Gap and General Albert Pike lay upon me.

The Ouachita Mountains of southwest Arkansas somehow seemed a welcoming site after my work of previous weeks. The spring breeze whispered through the tall pines, and I inhaled it deeply. I found the secluded cabin where I took the oath and made myself known to the sentries who allowed me entrance at once to the audience of General Pike.

"Hello, General."

"Do you make it a habit of murdering our agents in alleyways?"

"I'm sure I don't know what you mean."

"You're proving to be smarter than I ever believed you capable. Where did you hide the former contents of the mint building?"

I had been thinking about that inevitable question from Pike long before he asked it, and I decided to deny him that information. As long as I withheld the whereabouts of the stash, I could confidently expect to be kept alive, as K.G.C. assassins are less apt to murder one who knows the location of a vast treasure.

"General, I respectfully decline to mention the whereabouts of our plunder. You'll respect that I selected the choicest hiding spot in Louisiana, I'm sure."

"Yes, and now I see that you are proving to be *infinitely* smarter than I ever believed you to be. Your father would be proud."

"Father is dead."

"Yes, I heard."

"News seems to travel fast these days."

"Our network is vast and acts as a sponge in the collection and as a beacon in the communication of information crucial to our cause. Drouet, you *do* know that the booty you hid will be used to fund our agents in the field?"

"I am quite aware of that, General."

"Good, because you will distribute said resources to said agents across the country, along with private dispatches, as we deem necessary. You will begin soon."

"General, I explicitly told you of my intentions to return to General Watie and his forces in the Indian Nations once I fulfilled my duties in New Orleans. I will continue my work with The Circle when the war ends."

Pike smiled a devilish smile, one that I did not like.

"And return you will, Drouet. You will immediately return to the service of Confederate Brigadier General Stand Watie, a southern hero now called the Swamp Fox—and long-time clandestine agent of the Knights of the Golden Circle."

"Watie?"

"He has been with us since shortly after The Circle was formed. He believes in its founding principles."

"As I said to you before I left this cabin for New Orleans some many weeks previous, I am honored to fight by his side."

"Good. Now that I am no longer an official of the Confederate States of America, you will answer to Watie, not only in matters of war but also in matters related to The Circle, for now. Understood?"

"Understood. The Circle's network seems as vast as you have described."

"Drouet, when this war broke out, the cause of the Confederacy became the cause of our Circle, even if only briefly. But I am no longer an official of the Confederacy, and the Confederacy will eventually be no more, certainly so after the recent unfortunate events in New Orleans of which you witnessed firsthand. I have to now re-devote my energies to the cause of The Circle, a cause that helped ignite the war, to begin with."

Just then, I saw the dark outline of a shadow person in the corner of the room. It lingered for a moment longer than usual before dissolving into nothingness.

"Well, then, I stand ready to report to General Watie as soon as possible, General."

"Very good, Drouet."

I set out for the Indian Nations the following morning.

When I left the fighting Confederate Indians for New

Orleans a relatively short time before, I did so with a guilty conscience. Those men comprised a bold lot, and it did not feel right leaving their midst in the middle of a war. Nevertheless, I returned in time for the events mentioned earlier in this narrative—the Battle of Honey Springs, where we suffered defeat, and the successful captures of the *J.R. Williams* steamboat and the Federal supply wagon at Cabin Creek.

While the spoils of both those captures seemed unequal to the booty taken from the mint building, I enjoyed a certain excitement and exhilaration non-existent during the New Orleans heist, a fact due in large part to the bullets returned in our direction from the Yankee soldiers manning both vessels during said attacks.

Now, by 1864, General Watie had certainly heard the bleak news coming from the east, and he knew the Confederacy could not hold out much longer. As a top K.G.C. operative, he enjoyed constant dispatches through The Circle's vast network covering both the northern and southern sections of the country. I stood proud of assisting him and his forces. They fought on as aggressively as ever, attacking and raiding whenever and wherever possible.

Nevertheless, as a man of The Circle, Watie planned for the future, as per the purpose of the K.G.C. and General Pike by that time. Throughout what is now eastern Oklahoma, Watie and his men hid away much of the guns and ammunition seized from the aforementioned raids of 1864, and from other, smaller raids before and after.

By war's end, Watie had become acquainted with Jesse James, another ardent member of The Circle, through their mutual friend, General Pike. After Pike's release from Confederate military service, he spent every waking hour coordinating the activities of the K.G.C., recruiting new agents and coordinating the concealment of money and arms for future use.

James had suffered beatings at the hands of northern soldiers and watched as they tortured his stepfather, providing the former religion-filled, peace-loving farm boy with ample reason to hate Yankees wherever he found them. Further, his family owned six slaves who worked on the family hemp farm, providing Jesse with all the prerequisites necessary to join The Circle. In Jesse James, Pike found a perfect K.G.C. agent, marauder, and assassin.

Pike and Watie knew of James' guerrilla activities toward the end of the war. Those activities included, among other things, successful raids on Yankee steamboats and wagon trains in Arkansas, making his war résumé similar to that of General Stand Watie who made a living doing the same in Indian Territory.

One day in 1864, Watie summoned me to his tent. When I arrived, he welcomed me inside his quarters and showed me a recent dispatch from General Pike. The dispatch noted a recent conversation between Pike and George Bickley, a Cincinnati physician and *the* original founder of the Knights of the Golden Circle. Their conversation had centered around recent unfortunate turns of events for the Confederacy's war effort and the inevitable surrender to come. Both Bickley and Pike agreed that The Circle moved immediately into its post-war chapter, an era necessarily involving raids upon banks, trains, steamboats, ships, stagecoaches, and wagon trains to procure the money and materials needed to pursue the annexation of territories to comprise its desired slave-holding empire.

Bickley had suggested the Cincinnati-based Ohio and Mississippi railway as The Circle's prestigious first target. A resident of Cincinnati who had traveled via the Ohio and Mississippi line on many occasions, Bickley knew the line lacked essential security and stood as a sitting duck for war-seasoned raiders—looters such as Jesse James, Watie and myself. Bickley also knew the train carried multiple safes of the Adams Express Company, the ultimate object of the job.

Watie refused to gallivant off to rob an Ohio train while leaving his Cherokee Mounted Rifles alone with Yankees increasingly ever-present in the Indian Territory. That left the Ohio job to me and Mr. James, Watie said.

I met with Jesse and Frank James and their men outside Southwest City, Missouri barely a week later. I came upon their camp as the sun began to set.

"Hallo the camp!"

"Come in slowly with your hands in the air."

I walked in and gave the K.G.C. sign for recognition on the battlefield—that is, with hands open, palms touching and resting upon my head with fingers pointed forward. A man then stepped to within five feet of me and signaled his K.G.C. response by placing his open hands upon his shoulders where an epaulet is usually worn with elbows close to his side.

Staying within K.G.C. protocol for introductions among those who had never before met, he then uttered, "Are you a Knight of the Golden Circle?"

"I am."

"How am I to know you are a K.G.C.?"

"By my password."

"Will you give it to me?"

"I did not receive it, but I will letter it with you."

We then proceeded to spell out the password with him beginning with the first letter and me answering with the second, and so on.

"S."

"O."

"L."

"D."

"I."

"E."

"R."

"May I enter?"

"You may enter."

I immediately and silently counted those around the camp-fire and, with the addition of myself, the gang numbered fifteen.

The gazes of the gang members indicated a deep suspicion of me. They watched my every move as I found a place to stand by the fire. I began asking myself if I could survive the days ahead amongst this lot.

Shadow people lurked everywhere at the edge of the camp. I wondered what the shadowy figures watched and listened for.

The man with whom I had exchanged the K.G.C. signs and passwords introduced himself.

"I'm Frank James."

As soon as I introduced myself, we heard footsteps from the surrounding woods. Just then, one of their members emerged from the darkness and walked directly toward me.

"I'm Jesse James. I keep hearing about the coming surrender, but surrender has played out for good with me."

Those were the first words I ever heard uttered from the man, and I knew he meant them.

The number of the gang now stood at sixteen.

Jesse, Frank, and I discussed the war on into the night. I asked him if he thought the plunder from our various raids would suffice to fund a second Confederate uprising if it came to that.

"The Confederacy ain't dead yet. But let me tell you something—there're other funds coming in from places you wouldn't believe if I told you."

"Like from where?"

"Just leave it. I ain't authorized."

Those comments proved words on which to ponder.

Forty-four days later we arrived in the vicinity of Cincinnati but stayed on the Kentucky side of the river. We decided to use skiffs with which to cross the river. Jesse and I were the first to float across the river to begin surveying and planning for the job ahead. We walked a section of tracks between the stations of Gravel Pit and North Bend and found a spot where one pried rail from the track section would culminate in a derailed engine.

Two days later in the late afternoon, the entire gang arrived on the spot, removed said rail and waited. A short time after eight o'clock we heard the engine of the express train chugging down the tracks in our direction. It came into view, and we beheld the engine pulling the Adams Express car immediately behind with four passenger coaches and a baggage car following.

The engine roared past the missing rail, derailed and fell over on its side. The Adams Express car, which held the safes, capsized and its roof split wide open, with one of the safes rolling out to a spot more than convenient for our gunpowder men to blast it open. The passenger coaches and baggage car remained upright.

In an instant, our band sprang upon the cars. Two men approached each car with two more behind them to provide cover. Each member of the gang, except for myself, carried Navy revolvers and they commenced firing said weapons over the cars while demanding in the sharpest tones that the passengers and train personnel refrain from any defensive demonstrations lest they get their brains blown out.

Jesse and I ran to the Adams Express car with our gunpowder specialists to supervise the opening of the safes. We had planned for our men at the other cars to simply hold the engineer and passengers at bay long enough for our gunpowder men to blast open the safes.

Just then I heard one of our members declare, "Rob every damn man, but don't hurt the ladies!" My eyes scanned down the tracks and saw our men pouring into the passenger cars to loot the railway line's customers.

I looked over to Jesse and expressed my dissatisfaction at the turn of events.

"The K.G.C. is robbing citizens now, Jesse? Were these the orders?"

"Yes. And I gave 'em. Never you mind it and let's get these safes open."

The capsizing of the express car essentially imprisoned the messenger within. At the beginning, he poked his head out of an opening to ascertain the events outside. One of our gunpowder men, standing within five feet of the opening, saw the messenger, aimed his Navy at the target and told him to behave lest his exposed head explode to Kingdom Come.

So, while my group went about the business of blowing open the steel safes of the Adams Express, our men in the passenger cars commenced robbing the male travelers of pocketbooks, gold watches, diamond pins, gold rings, bracelets, coins – both gold and silver -- and paper money. One of our associates even broke off the gold handle of a man's walking cane and stuffed it into his own pocket.

During all of this, the conductor attempted to offer resistance. One of our men commenced firing upon him but, thankfully, missed his target.

From time to time during the affair, I looked down at the passenger car spectacle and liked none of it. I planned to separate myself from the band shortly after we crossed the river back into Kentucky. In the midst of this affair which I had, in my mind, deemed a debacle, I longed for the feel of a glass of Sazerac in my hand and the sweetness of its nectar on my lips in far more comfortable environs and with better society.

Safes finally blown open, we emptied the contents which amounted to thirty thousand dollars in U.S. government bonds. Frank and Jesse secured these in water-proof pouches for the skiff ride across the river.

Bonds secured and passengers robbed, we traversed the river for the last time and ran like hell for our horses that were stabled at a farm owned by a K.G.C. sympathizer a few miles distant. The horses were saddled, fresh and ready to go. From there, we made for Verona, Kentucky where we picked up a new set of fresh horses hidden away at the home of another K.G.C. sympathizer.

While we tarried not at the man's home, we listened as he offered up a quick round of news and rumors circulating throughout the country.

"Any of you men ever hear of Loreta Velazquez, our lady spy?"

I remained quiet, but all amongst our band said they had heard the remarkable stories of Madame Velazquez, the rebel secret agent loved by Southerners and despised by those in the north.

OUR HOST ELABORATED FURTHER.

"Heard she was killed by a certain Mrs. Williams who'd been working for the Federals. Velazquez had been recruiting and organizing our boys in gray across the country, had even been organizing a rebellion of Confederate prisoners held in Ohio and Indiana. Yankees wanted her dead and paid another woman to do it."

Hearing this news felt like a ton of bricks had fallen upon me.

I asked how this information had been verified.

"Them photographer men recorded it. Saw a picture of it. Showed her shot up body lying there on the ground."

Jesse spoke up.

"I hear she spent a lot of time down in New Orleans. Did you ever know her, Broussard?"

"Heard the name, sure. But never met her."

Frank and Jesse said they were bound for the town of Cynthiana, Kentucky where a man with the last name of Stamper had another set of fresh horses as well as instructions on where to take the bonds now owned by The Circle. The route to Cynthiana took the band further east than I wanted to travel with a band that robbed citizens, so I lied and stated to the group that my instructions called for an immediate return to General Stand Watie in the Indian Territory. Frank and Jesse admired Watie and possessed at least some respect for the K.G.C. hierarchy, so they seemed to have confidence in the story.

The time lay upon me.

I made straight for Louisville, then down through western Kentucky, across the southern tip of Indiana into Tennessee, angling directly back to Watie and my duties in the Indian Nations.

Therein explains my role in the North Bend Train Robbery still "unsolved," an event that stands as the first train robbery in the history of the United States, as the first of such raids by the K.G.C., as the model for The Circle's future holdups, and as the first non-war related stickup involving Frank and Jesse James—all at once.

8

A CURIOUS STRANGER IN INDIAN TERRITORY

SOME FIFTY DAYS AFTER THE TRAIN ROBBERY NEAR Cincinnati, I found myself back in the land of the Five Civilized Tribes of eastern Indian Territory. Having traveled the entire distance with Loreta heavy on my mind, I returned in time to see the war out with General Watie and his men right up to Watie's surrender in Doaksville on June 23, 1865, some two months after Lee's surrender at Appomattox.

News traveled slowly in those days.

I did not know of Lee's surrender on April 9 until returning to Indian Territory. The news gave me to know that the Ohio train robbery on May 5 happened squarely after war's end, surely making the K.G.C. action there against civilians a non-war affair that could land the participants in prison for a long time.

I also did not know of another great event that took place barely one week after Lee's surrender—the assassination of Abraham Lincoln by the young and distinguished actor, John Wilkes Booth on April 14.

Why did that name ring a bell? I thought to myself at the

time. The answer came suddenly. Because I had heard Father mention the name on multiple occasions.

Then, I remembered, once again, other words from Father, words uttered by him when I asked about leaving The Circle: "Just slither within its ranks as unnoticed as possible, play the game, play it smart, wait it out until the end, and, when the end comes, as it most certainly will come, have yourself situated on the other side of the world if possible."

As it turned out, I failed to heed his advice. Both the end of the war and Lincoln's assassination occurred with me working a train robbery in Ohio with Jesse and Frank James, all of us in the service of the K.G.C., the very society responsible for the "Killing of the King" at Ford's Theatre in Washington City— hardly the behavior of one slithering within K.G.C. ranks as unnoticed as possible.

I longed to return to New Orleans, to the Pickwick, to the dark and shadowy streets of the Vieux Carre, and, if by some seemingly unlikely chance she still lived, to Loreta Janeta Velazquez. New Orleans certainly did not qualify as "the other side of the world," but I knew how to navigate it and felt comfortable in its clutches, even if hordes of blue-coats now roamed its wicked back alleys and side streets.

After Watie earned the distinction of becoming the last Confederate General to surrender to the Yankees in late June, he and his men remained in the Choctaw Nation for a short time, and I remained with them.

One evening a few hours before sundown, Watie called me to his tent. I went straightaway, ready to receive orders not from a Confederate General but from a K.G.C. superior. I somehow knew this meeting would prove my last with the cunning fighter. I entered the tent and paid my salute.

"It has been an honor to fight alongside you, Broussard. A damned fine honor."

"And vice versa, General. You have taught me a lot. I'm forever grateful."

"We were clever, devious, bold and decisive, and those things took us far. You possessed those qualities in spades when first I met you. But the fight continues, and that's why I called you here."

"Yes, sir?"

"I've been messaged to order you back to New Orleans at once. You leave first thing in the morning."

"I cannot pretend for that to be anything other than the best of news, General."

"I hear you like a place there called the Pickwick Club."

"News does travel, General."

"After you return, you are to check in there regularly."

"That will not be a problem, sir. But, why?"

"You will receive dispatches there. If you are not handed an envelope while there, then there is no dispatch to be handed. You may go many months and not receive anything. Do we have an understanding?"

"Certainly, General."

"Good. You leave at dawn."

I saluted the General for the last time and then turned and exited. Barely an inch past the threshold of the tent's entryway I nearly collided with one making his own way to the General, one verily surrounded by a host of shadow people, and one-off whose lips flowed quick-fired prose appropriate to the situation.

"But as the unthought-on accident is guilty to what we wildly do, so we profess ourselves to be the slaves of chance, and flies of every wind that blows."

"I, too, like *The Winter's Tale*. To whom may I thank for such prose in the wilds of the Choctaw Nation on this summer night?"

Slowly, gracefully, he raised his hand.

"To thine own self be true, and it must follow, as the night the day, thou canst not then be false to any man. My name is John St. Helen, at your service."

Before me stood a man of worried expression and penetrating black eyes, a man whose physical countenance and mannerisms indicated genteel birth and upbringing and superior education. Despite his appearance of high culture, I felt his soft manners did little to hide the face of one capable of inflicting swift violence and certain death. He appeared only a few years older than me.

While he appeared somewhat disheveled, as if recently off a long trip, perhaps in the wild where attention to appearance is often difficult at best, nothing about his visage suggested he belonged anywhere in the vicinity of what then constituted the wilds of the western frontier.

"And I am Drouet Broussard, sir."

At that, St. Helen bowed, raised again and then stood silent, if only for a few seconds, his brain appearing to digest the few words I had just expressed, most notably the two comprising my name. I sensed he had heard those words before. He smiled.

"Strong reasons make strong actions, and you appear as one on a mission."

"I leave the company of General Watie and his Cherokee Mounted Rifles first thing in the morning."

"To where, pray?"

"To home. To New Orleans."

"Ah, I know the city well, Broussard!"

We shook hands, and he bade me adieu.

"Farewell, Drouet Broussard! God knows when we shall meet again."

St. Helen turned and into General Watie's tent he walked, and with a limp I noted.

I arose early the following morning to begin my voyage home. Barely out of Watie's camp, I turned around for one last look at the camp of men making up the Mounted Rifles. From out of one of the tents walked St. Helen, freshly-shaven, and carrying himself with the same elegant manner as the night before, albeit with the conspicuous hitch in his walk.

Of all those I had met since last leaving New Orleans, St. Helen stood out as the only one with whom I wanted to converse over a glass of Sazerac.

9

NEW ORLEANS UNDER COVER OF DARKNESS

WHILE EN ROUTE FROM INDIAN TERRITORY BACK TO THE Crescent City I allowed my mustache and beard to grow in. I wanted to walk the streets of home incognito, as no one there had ever seen me unshaven.

Once in New Orleans, I remained mindful that K.G.C. operatives wanted to stay apprised of my every move. The memory of the nighttime alleyway technicians stood as a constant reminder that people above me in The Circle most certainly desired to know the whereabouts of the mint heist plunder, and worried not over the methods necessary to pluck said information from yours truly.

More than a few high-ranking members of New Orleans society belonged to The Circle, and some within the ranks surely wanted answers regarding the hiding place. Even though I owned a respected name as the son of a prominent New Orleans businessman who helped establish the underground league, I knew I walked the streets of the Crescent City at my own risk.

While the fact that I alone knew the location of the cache

provided me a certain level of protection against K.G.C. assassins, there surely existed those more than willing to use whatever creative devices to make me chirp.

General Pike at least pretended an air of nonchalance over the matter and outwardly acted as if he believed in my stated commitment to using the booty toward the stated goals of the clandestine institution. What he truly thought of my intentions regarding the stash I knew not, but I actually possessed no certain designs of any kind regarding it.

Father had suggested I slither as unnoticed as possible while working within the society, sort of playing things by ear and keeping my options open, and that is exactly how I thought about the contents of the crypt at Lafayette Cemetery.

On my first night back home, a thick fog enveloped the city. Shadow people danced in and out of it. Over time, I came to the conclusion that these manifestations were fueled by dubious energies.

I went first to Father's old place and found that it had been ransacked thoroughly, probably by those looking for the loot or at least for clues to its whereabouts. I wondered about beautiful Marguerite but felt certain she had been safe while residing elsewhere in my absence. While there, I trimmed my new mustache and beard and made myself presentable to polite society. From there, I made straight for the apartment in the Vieux Carre. There I found more disarray, for each room had been completely plundered.

What the K.G.C. thugs did not find in my absence from New Orleans they undoubtedly hoped to discover with my return, another reminder for me to stay hidden in the shadows.

I cleaned up and made straightaway for the Pickwick. Nothing could dissuade me from a glass of Sazerac after so many months without one, not even a foggy night replete with shadow people.

There were clear reminders everywhere that as I strode the side streets and narrow alleyways of New Orleans I did so as a wanted man, not by the law or by the loud, ill-mannered and boisterous Yankees, but by a power higher than either, by a force that enlisted spies, informants, and thugs from the ranks of each.

The doorman at the Pickwick asked for my cape, but I politely refused to turn it over. The blades in the long pockets could function well within the Pickwick as well as out, and so the need for quick defense regardless of location won out over manners and etiquette.

I declined my favorite section on the second floor and chose a table on the first near the outer door against the possible necessity of a quick exit. Glass of Sazerac in hand, I began weighing over my next move.

I resolved two items immediately.

I could not reside at either of the night's previously-visited addresses without fear of capture whilst asleep and torture once awakened. Furthermore, I could not safely and confidently walk the streets without some sort of disguise.

Through the smoke and faint lighting, I saw a figure walk into the room and take a seat at the wall opposite me. A closer, more focused glance revealed a bearded Yankee officer. How he gained admittance into the Pickwick—a members-only club—I knew not, but then reminded myself that officers of occupying armies seldom asked permission in such matters. The blue-coat removed his hat, pulled a perfecto from his pocket, bit off the end, and promptly lit the tobacco-filled cylinder into action. In a matter of seconds, smoke bellowed from the table. While making as if minding my own business, I occasionally glanced his direction and soon ascertained beyond a shadow of a doubt that the set of eyes behind the camouflage of smoke were set intently on me. I remained seated for perhaps another thirty minutes and never once did those eyes between the smoke plumes cease peering straight at me.

Placing both hands in either pocket of my long cape, I arose and began my exit, first passing the Yankee officer before stepping through the door. His eyes remained intently upon me and gave me no welcome sign. In fact, they seemed to motion toward the door and away. I then stepped out into the thick fog of St. Charles Avenue.

,I stood momentarily, pondering my next steps and hoping my feet would lead me to a safe harbor.

My earlier thoughts contemplated paying a visit to the Velazquez residence on Prytania Street, but I declined that option for a couple of reasons. The same K.G.C. operatives interested in my whereabouts undoubtedly knew of her involvement in the mint heist and had probably ransacked her home on the same day they pillaged Father's properties, and those same agents most assuredly watched over her home on a regular basis to see who came and went, just as they unquestionably observed the two Broussard addresses for the same reason. Also, I certainly did not want to jeopardize any of her staff remaining in the home by serving as bait for such a villainous lot. For those same reasons, I could not reside with any friends or family, however distant.

While sitting inside the Pickwick, I considered the matter painstakingly while observing the set of piercing eyes in the smoke.

Finally, I chose the only alternative available to me; an unlikely hideout made all the more so if I remained there in disguise—Maggie Thompson's brothel on Customhouse Street in the red-light district not too many blocks distant if she would have me.

Father met Maggie some years before and made a life-long friend when he did, but few if any knew of the close association. Not only did he play in her well-known poker room on a regular basis but he also kept her out of trouble with various city fathers and even loaned her money during hard times. I knew her to be an honest, straight shooter and figured she might do me a favor out of respect for Father if for nothing else.

I reached the address on Customhouse, knocked and soon enjoyed the welcome smile of a young, beautiful, uniformed black lady who motioned me inside. Nothing much had changed within the foyer since my last visit some years before. Paintings, some by renowned artists, adorned the walls. On either side of the ornate oak doorway into the inner rooms hung French mirrors with gilt frames.

Maggie ran a tight ship, and one followed her protocol while on the premises. Steady clients were brought into a drawing room where they were expected to buy wine for everyone present. Strangers were escorted to a smaller room and interviewed by Maggie, while the two conversed over a glass of wine. If the stranger's credentials passed muster, then Maggie brought him into a drawing room and presented him by the first name to the assorted ladies of the house. If he found one of the ladies to his liking, he informed Maggie who, in turn, notified the strumpet who quietly slipped away to her boudoir and made ready for her suitor. The going rate for the adventure stood at fifteen dollars in those days. If Maggie made herself available for a particularly distinguished gentleman, the price stood at fifty dollars an hour plus liberal purchases of wine for assorted other guests throughout the night.

The petite door greeter knew me as a stranger and escorted me to the small drawing room at once. After a few minutes, Maggie walked in, sat down in a chair adjacent mine, poured the wine and then looked into my eyes.

"And who might I ask do I have the pleasure of meeting this night?"

"It's me, Maggie. Drouet Broussard."

She examined me thoroughly from top to bottom, but mostly she looked at my now bearded face and squarely into my eyes.

"I can't believe it. In my mind's eye, you are a boy, yet you are your father's boy, and you are certainly grown up!"

"I wondered if you would recognize me."

"I heard you fought in the war up in the Indian Territory. Your father told me a few stories. I'm sorry he is gone now."

"It's true. I did. And the reason Father told you those stories is because he knew you to be a lady of utmost discretion in all things."

Her eyes welled as she thought of Father, and the sight of it made my eyes nearly do the same, for she and Father were the closest and most trusted of friends and he visibly remained in her heart.

"That's why I'm here tonight, Maggie. I'm in a trouble of sorts, and I need your help."

"I know it isn't a lady of mine you need. You could have your pick from most any in our entire fair city."

"I need shelter and concealment."

"My home is your home. Use as you deem best."

She stood as if to start for the drawing room. I rose, as well.

I then pressed close to Maggie from behind, and as she turned toward me, I placed a hand at her waist and kissed her on the cheek.

"I am indebted to you and your kindness."

"You, Broussard, slay me. You know I will give you anything you want."

"I will pay you handsomely. There are those who await my return to Father's home and to his apartment, and they wish me no goodwill should they lay their hands upon me. Your place will provide me a haven in which to hide for a time in disguise while I devise ways to confront my enemies on my own terms."

"You can have anything within these walls, Drouet. And I mean anything."

"I won't forget that, but I will pay above and beyond. I come and go at all hours of the day and night, and I will pay for the inconvenience."

"I have a room for you, a nice one down the hall from mine."

"Do you still entertain at the poker room where Father lost so much money over the years?"

Maggie laughed.

"No man showed more grace while losing money. Yes, every Friday and Saturday night and sometimes during the week. Do you play?"

"I'm afraid I own more than a few of Father's bad habits."

Maggie smiled deviously.

"I don't trust a man without any. I will inform my doormen to let you come and go as you please. You are completely safe here."

Over the next several weeks, I became acquainted with the ladies and staff of the house, further cultivated the beard and mustache, and altered to a certain degree my wardrobe. While keeping a long cape in which to conceal my blades, I began wearing a black, planters style hat.

On Friday and Saturday nights I worked to hone my poker skills in Maggie's poker room. I hadn't need of the winnings when they came. I played only to socialize, to meet people and to gather news about town. Naturally, our Yankee friends had discovered Maggie's place and the rest of the red-light district soon after taking the city in 1862. Many were the blue coats who lost their money at the poker tables and their virginity in the boudoirs within the dimly-lit houses along Customhouse Street in those days.

There came a night when I enjoyed a long and successful roll at the table. The night started with me taking money from Yankee boys who seemed to inevitably lose whatever card-playing skills they might possess when they were distracted by the never-ending music, laughter, dancing and the clinking of crystal as the spirits flowed freely. As the night progressed and the young boys in blue left defeated, their seats at the table were filled by players with considerably greater skill, but my success continued unabated as I employed the time-honored methods of scores of poker players before me; when faced with equal or greater talent—I cheated.

Many were the piles of coinage and paper I raked in throughout the night, and I considered playing a few more hands only to give back some of the spoils I had taken from a couple of players who stood at the precipice of poker bank-ruptcy and embarrassment. I considered this not out of any sense of honor, but as a device to prevent any unfortunate scenes in Maggie's place.

By then, a sizable crowd had gathered around the table. I played a few more hands and contemplated retiring for the evening when into the room walked a bearded Yankee officer. I knew him as the same perfecto-smoking blue coat from my last visit at the Pickwick. From the doorway, he cast his gaze immediately upon me while cupping both hands over his pistol grips.

Just then, one of the bluecoats amongst the crowd greeted him.

"Welcome, Colonel Snider."

The man addressed as Colonel Snider acknowledged the greeting with a slight nod of the head, all while holding those grips and keeping both eyes directed straight at me.

The player opposite me at the table whispered, "That's

Colonel Thomas Snider. Someone said he's the one who paid that Yankee woman to kill Loreta Velazquez, that lady spy."

Others at the table and in the room noticed his continued stare at me, his ready firearms, and a feeling of disconcertedness fell upon the scene. I maintained as best I could a poker face, winning first one hand and losing another.

Snider seemed to edge closer to my immediate vicinity with each passing hand, and I contemplated my next move in light of the situation. Just as I reached down to touch my own pistol grips and feel the handles of both blades concealed in my cape, Snider removed the cigar from his mouth and bellowed out his orders.

"I want everyone to clear out of here, now!"

Members of the crowd and players at the table began departing the scene post haste. I pocketed my winnings, placed my hat topside and made as if to rise. The Colonel issued his last order while continuing his gaze upon yours truly.

"You stay where you are."

Snider and I were then alone in the room, and he closed the door.

"I have you now, Drouet Broussard."

10

BEGINNING LIFE AFTER THE WAR

THE YANKEE COLONEL STOOD BEFORE ME WITH THE barrels of both his sidearms aimed in my direction as the ever-present laughter, music, and revelry echoed throughout the premises. *This is funny*, I thought, given that I faced a grim current state of affairs.

"Drouet, how do you tolerate this?"

"This what, Colonel?"

"The sights, the sounds, the aroma of indulgence everywhere here."

"Quite easily, I can assure you."

At that, the Colonel peeled away the mustache, beard and grotesque pork chop sideburns peculiar to Yankee military men, to reveal for the second dramatic time in our friendship, Loreta Velazquez.

I sat frozen and nearly unable to conceal my astonishment at her most recent deception.

She quickly smiled and cleared her throat to indicate an upcoming change back to her feminine voice.

"I, too, rather enjoy the sights, sounds and aroma here,

delightful manifestations of decadence, Drouet. I completely understand why you live here."

I know I stood silent and somewhat spellbound for longer than I wanted. Loreta had completely hoodwinked me for the second time with her disguises, and I stood in awe of her ability and still do.

"Another thing, Drouet, please explain your pitiful excuse for a disguise. I've watched you for the last week and immediately saw right through the planter's hat, beard, and mustache. I need to train you in the art of disguise."

"How did you know it was me?"

"Your eyes, Drouet. They give you away, I'm afraid."

"My God, Loreta. It's really you. I truly believed it when I heard you had been killed."

"I'm sorry you had to hear that. But we're both here, together again. Pray, what mischief lies ahead for us now that you have arrived?"

"Arrived?"

"Here. To this place, to this brothel where you belong, achieving the aim which is the highest in your life. I am glad to see you so happy, and I know that there is nothing else that anyone can do for you because you have risen so high in the world."

Then, she removed her Yankee Colonel's hat and made a grand bow.

"That's real funny, Loreta. But I'm here for a damned good reason, and you look kind of funny yourself bedecked in your Yankee get up."

She laughed.

"Colonel Snider just made his last appearance, as his was only a temporary engagement, one week long to be exact."

"And why is that?"

"Do you forget that Yankees run this town? Impersonate a

Yankee long enough and someone wearing blue will ask for documentation, for your background, for a solid story, and it had better check out when they do."

"Yes, I get the general idea."

"So, when did you hear about my murder?"

"Not that very long ago up in Kentucky, and it sounded as if the story had been retold everywhere north and south of the Mason-Dixon Line for quite some time when I heard it. Even a few minutes ago at this very poker table, someone whispered out of your earshot that Colonel Snider—meaning you, the Yankee officer who had just pranced into the room—paid the Yankee woman to kill Loreta Velazquez. Just what the hell actually happened?"

"I got the rumor started while masquerading as a one Mrs. Williams after hearing my real name mentioned one too many times in association with certain nefarious activities with which I had no actual involvement. It's bad enough knowing my real guilt in a number of actual shenanigans, but I seek no reputation on the back of crimes not involving me at all. I mentioned the murder of Velazquez to a group of well-placed gentlemen at a poker table one night, and the false story spread like wildfire. For the longest time, Yankee authorities actually bought the story."

"But I heard there was a photograph showing a one Loreta Velazquez lying dead on the ground full of bullet holes."

"Drouet, surely you know never to believe everything you hear and not even everything you see. I am the one who placed the photograph of that poor unfortunate and unknown woman into circulation."

"Loreta, you truly are brilliant...fostering the news of your own demise! I have to hear more of your adventures."

"In time I shall recount more. But, tonight let us retire to your quarters here, wherever that is."

I took Loreta by the hand, exited the poker room and made for my room downstairs.

"Follow me to all the comforts of home."

As soon as the door to my room shut, I drew her hungrily into my arms.

The following day, Loreta began telling me of her exploits on behalf of the K.G.C. around the country, narratives that kept me enthralled at every turn. No other woman I had ever known owned her daring, cunning, beauty and charm. I knew at that moment I would never meet her like again and vowed then and there to never let her go.

Shortly after leaving New Orleans when we had completed the mint heist mission, Loreta flattened her breasts with braces and wire shields, donned a man's wig, fake mustache, and beard, and successfully began playing the part of Harry T. Buford, Confederate lieutenant. She padded her arms to appear more muscular, smoked cigars and walked with a masculine gait and successfully passed herself off as a bonafide Confederate officer. As Buford, she raised a battalion for the Confederacy out of the state of Arkansas and, at times, found herself in actual battles on numerous occasions.

Loreta grew tired of regular duty, began lobbying for a position as a Confederate spy and, with the help of her K.G.C. contacts, earned a role sending her back and forth across the country gaining valuable information for Confederate generals and the government in Richmond. Oftentimes, the information she gathered concerned Yankee troop movements.

During her travels north, Loreta gained the confidence of Yankee officials and eventually secured a role in the Yankees' National Detective Bureau, a move that made her a double agent, but one always fighting tenaciously and exclusively for the Southern Cause.

I listened with rapt attention as she recounted the details of her activities in those years after the mint heist, especially those undertakings while in the employ of the National Detective Bureau. Her stories gave me to know how deftly her covert actions would have met the approval of Father, whose words regarding slithering about incognito kept ringing true.

Through a clandestine, complicated and treacherous web, oftentimes in the midst of enemy players in their own land, Loreta glided as if a bird on the wind. From my own K.G.C. and Confederate contacts, I often heard bits and pieces of news related to her work. I knew she had played a pivotal role while in Memphis assisting General Forrest while also helping to lead Yankee General Washburn astray with false intelligence related to troop movements.

Loreta knew that the goals of the Confederacy had become, for all intents and purposes, the same as those of the K.G.C. and believed that she assisted both organizations by simply making herself available for assignments, however dangerous, during the war. She eventually wrote a book about her many adventures as a double agent working for the Confederacy, but I have it on the highest authority that, within the tome, she intentionally scrambled dates and chronology in order to protect persons throughout the country still living.

Whatever inaccuracies lie within those pages are by her own design.

Naturally, I wanted to learn all I could about her missions during those years following our work together in New Orleans.

"I heard that you possibly helped General Forrest while up in Memphis. How did you get involved in that and how did it play out?"

"While staying in Mobile, I received a note written in a masculine hand requesting I meet the writer that evening in the nearby square. I met the gentleman who turned out to be Lieutenant Shorter of Arkansas."

"How did Shorter know of you?"

"Probably from officials he worked with. He also knew about my ability to disguise myself when needed. Shorter said he had recently captured a Yankee spy belonging to the command of General Hurlbut. From that spy, Shorter retrieved a paper containing highly accurate accounts of the movements of General Forrest and other Confederates.

"Shorter changed the paper's accounts so as to throw the Yankees on the wrong scent. My charge, if I accepted it, was to take the paper to Memphis and deliver it to Yankee General Washburn."

"I bet you concocted a great disguise to help with this, yes?"

"I definitely had to pretend to be somebody I wasn't, and so, yes, a slight disguise proved helpful. I decided to go by the name of Mrs. Williams, which was the name of my deceased husband. Yes, Drouet, I have been married before.

"I had to convince General Washburn that I obtained the paper from the spy before he was captured by Shorter. Shorter also had a dispatch he wanted me to deliver to a Confederate agent in Memphis, a dispatch that the agent would then get into the hands of General Forrest. Shorter gave me instructions on where to find this agent, as well as a description of his appearance and a password proving to the spy that I could be trusted."

"Loreta, had those Yankees found on your person the dispatch meant for the Confederate spy they would have hung you."

"Well, Shorter stressed that this was a sensitive and important mission and that if I were found with the dispatch then, yes, the game would be over for me—and for good.

"Like I said, Shorter had heard of my prowess in assuming

disguises and suggested I adopt the dress of a poor country woman fleeing to Yankee lines for protection.

"I agreed to accept the mission and was, right then and there, given a horse, pistol and ninety dollars. I was instructed to use the weapon only as a last resort and to absolutely not carry it into Yankee lines to see General Washburn. It was feared that the presence of a firearm on my person might arouse suspicions and deem me untrustworthy to the Yankees or give me away altogether."

"So, you mounted the horse and made your way to Memphis?"

"I did. I made it to the Yankee lines with very little trouble. I made sure to hide away the pistol before encountering any Yankee soldiers. I hid it away in an unlocked church nearby. I eventually happened upon an inquisitive Yankee lieutenant who asked about the nature of my business. I answered that I had very important papers to deliver to General Washburn.

"The lieutenant asked from where had I obtained the papers, and I replied that I hailed from Holly Springs and that a gentleman there gave me one hundred dollars to get the papers through to General Washburn.

"The lieutenant asked me the name of the gentleman and what did he look like, but I replied that my instructions were to get the papers delivered to the good General and not to give away the name and appearance of the gentleman back in Holly Springs.

"The young lieutenant seemed to believe my story but said getting to see Washburn was not so easy to do at that particular moment and then proceeded to obtain for me a first-rate breakfast. He also asked about Confederate troop movements from whence I came, and I claimed to have seen a large force of them near Holly Springs which was far from the truth.

"To make a long story short, I made it to General Washburn with the help of the young lieutenant, and the papers were delivered."

"Why is it I get the feeling you won over the lieutenant in more ways than one?"

"Well, the lieutenant seemed to fancy himself a possible suitor to the poor country woman I portrayed, paying heed to my every need as we made our way to Washburn, even putting me in the nicest private lodgings at his own expense and making me accept money from him with which to purchase better clothes."

"I'll bet he had to twist your arm."

"Funny. I figured the benefits gained at the lieutenant's expense were simply the spoils of the greater game in which we were all involved and accepted with the appreciative smile of a poor country woman.

"So, having seen the papers delivered to Washburn, and while staying in the Memphis hotel on the lieutenant's generosity, I decided to slip out one night and pay a visit to the Confederate spy residing not too far away from the hotel so as to complete the second half of my mission.

"In a very short time, I made it to the address given me and knocked on the door. The agent answered, and he proved to look almost exactly as he had been described to me. I uttered the password and he then eagerly drew me inside and inquired as to the purpose of my visit. I gave him the information to be delivered to General Forrest, and he explained it would be delivered to him at once.

"During the course of our conversation, he learned about the young and adoring Yankee lieutenant and asked if I would attempt to extract from him certain troop movements much in need by our Confederates thereabouts. I replied that I most certainly would—and I did, having the information to the agent on the very next day—but that I did not feel safe coming back to his residence for fear of being discovered by my admiring lieutenant and his cadre of officers who would gladly see me hung if they learned my true purpose.

"We both agreed that I would write down the information on a piece of paper and hide it at a certain location where he could retrieve it. As I said, I got the needed information from the lieutenant, jotted it down, and then hid it away for our agent.

"The lieutenant gave me everything I needed to know about the number and position of Yankee forces along the Memphis and Charleston Railroad and that the force at Colliersville was being strengthened as we spoke in anticipation of an attack there.

"After learning the news of Forrest's raid, I made as if frightened among my Yankee acquaintances in Memphis, expressing fears that Forrest might execute a raid on the city of Memphis and capture me. The doting lieutenant and his Yankee friends believed my acting job and assured me I was safe in their hands. Of course, Forrest did not raid Memphis, but he slipped by them after a somewhat lengthy campaign while securing enough cattle and assorted other booty to more than reward him for the trouble.

"Drouet, I was so proud of myself after what I accomplished on that job. You would have been excited and proud to have seen me in action. I successfully saw the false papers delivered to Washburn, delivered the needed information to our Confederate agent in Memphis in the dark of night, all while gaining for him Yankee troop information, a task above and beyond the scope of my original charge!"

"You are quite remarkable, Loreta. I stand in awe. You were born to this work of deception."

"Oh, but there is more, Drouet—so much more!"

"Pray, don't let me stop you. I want to hear everything. Give me the best stories first."

"I know you're indulging me, Drouet, and that you were involved in enough of your own shenanigans since the mint heist. I want to hear all about it."

"All in due course. Pray, continue."

"You won't believe that I was tasked by the Yankees to capture the notorious lady spy."

"Which one? There were several."

"A one Loreta Janeta Velazquez."

"Ha! And who assigned you this momentous charge?"

Before she answered, Loreta smiled proudly as if to say "You won't believe what I am about to tell you."

And then she told me.

"Lafayette Baker, head of Lincoln's National Detective Bureau."

I admit, as her words began penetrating my brain, I almost doubted their validity, but as they sank in further, I swiftly allowed that Loreta could pull off such an amazing feat of infiltration if anyone could.

"Well, thankfully, it looks as if you failed in that mission! Pray, my dear, please proceed."

"I went to the north for a time to visit my brother who was being held in a Yankee prison. Seeing our many Southern boys who had been captured on the battlefield reinforced my feelings of intense dislike for their captors. I established in my mind that these blue-bellies were not so smart that I could not successfully infiltrate their ranks in the Yankee capital itself.

"I determined to make for Washington City and, while visiting some friends there I had known before the war, work to meet those in the city who could assist me in my work."

Oh, how I admired the audacity of this woman!

"I found my old friends, both working in the employ of the Yankee military, one a general and one a captain."

"Who were these officers?"

Loreta gave me the identities of both men, but I uphold her wishes in keeping their names forever buried, lest they pay today for their inadvertent support to the lady rebel spy back then.

"I began socializing to some degree with both officials, but the general seemed most glad to see me and pay me continual attention. Naturally, he wanted to know about all my adventures since we had last met.

"Oh, I have to also tell you that both these Yankee gentlemen knew me as Mrs. Williams, the name of my deceased husband. They also knew that I am of Spanish extraction and that most all of my family resided at that time in Cuba and in Spain.

"Both men had known my late husband, but neither knew that he had passed while in Confederate military service at the very outbreak of the war. I told the general that my husband had northern sympathies and that after his death I had been plundered by the hated rebels and decided to come north where I had resided for some time.

"And, so, it was through the general that I met Lafayette Baker of the National Detective Bureau.

"Upon meeting Mr. Baker, I quickly ascertained him to be a first-rate thug and a second-rate detective, one willing to use whatever means at his disposal, legal or illegal, to extract information from a man. He seemed willing to use whatever devices necessary to rise to the top and to draw into his possession as much personal wealth as possible. He was not at all content with who he was or with his place in the world. I took him as being a man of average intelligence at best, and one who, if given ample clues, still stood ill-equipped in procuring valuable information for the Yankee war department.

"On the very night that the general introduced me to Baker, I recounted to him the ruse of a story about my late husband succumbing to an untimely death right at the war's beginning, but in the service of the northern army, not the Confederate. Neither the general nor Baker had any way of knowing that my husband had actually died while as a rebel officer very early on in the late conflict.

"Luckily, my story was reinforced by the general who introduced us, a fact which put me in good stead with Colonel Baker at the outset. I told Colonel Baker that my position since my husband's passing had been precarious, having lost everything through the rebellion and that I desired employment of any capacity in his detective corps.

"I told him I had traveled extensively throughout the South and knew many prominent people there upon whom I sought revenge for my predicament. Baker asked me many questions, some about my motives, some about previous employment and a host of other matters. I answered each of his queries quickly and with enough apparent frankness that I felt I had made a good impression upon him, as well as on my friend the general who stood by during the entire conversation. As I said before, the general was so thoroughly impressed with me that he advocated my case in the strongest of terms to Colonel Baker then and there.

"Colonel Baker said he would think the matter over, that he did not know if he had any open positions at present, and that is how he left it.

"So, I went about my business, leaving Washington City when I needed to call on my Confederate contacts, and then returning to Washington City when those calls were completed.

"Over a course of time, I called upon Colonel Baker at his office and furnished him a number of bits of information of no real value, but which nonetheless aided him in breaking up fraudulent practices and bringing certain criminals in his own department to justice.

"Baker was average at sniffing out corruption in the various bureaux under his direction and even in other government agencies in Washington City, but barely adequate in purging the corruption once he had been made aware of it. Much to his chagrin, however, he received nothing but scorn and no accolades for pursuing the criminals, as the corruption ran deep and with the full knowledge and some participation of those whose charge it was to prosecute such.

"The Colonel seemed to become more favorably impressed with me as time went by and I knew in my heart he would eventually find me a position in his corps—and he did!

"And that was his mistake...he had been taken in, and by a woman. I began my work in his detective bureau and watched him as he exposed corruption in his own department and in other areas of Lincoln's government. Limited as he was, he rooted out rascals throughout Washington City once made aware of them. Unfortunately for him, these scoundrels had protectors in the Congress and other high places, and the very people who had secured his services on behalf of the government now officially sought to destroy him.

"But none of that was my concern. Now, as a double agent, I went to work for the detective bureau and successfully completed numerous missions similar to those undertaken in Memphis, as well as infiltrating the Yankee treasury department."

Mention of subverting the treasury department sounded unbelievable even to me. Both Loreta and myself had fruitfully completed numerous missions, together and separately, against sizeable odds, but penetrating the treasury department in Washington City stood as an almost impossible task.

I leaned toward her.

"I have to hear about this, Loreta."

"You will. One day as I sat in Colonel Baker's office, he told me he had a special assignment for me and would I be interested? I answered as I usually did, in the affirmative, but requesting the details. I will never forget his exact words:

"I want you to find this woman who is traveling and figuring as a Confederate agent. Some of my people have been on her track for a long time, but she is a slippery customer, and they have never been able to lay hands on her."

"I knew beyond a shadow of a doubt he spoke of me, especially when he commenced speaking of some of my movements on behalf of the Confederacy while away from Washington City. I felt particularly vulnerable at that moment and wanted more than anything to be out of his office and out of Washington City.

"I 'accepted' only as a ruse to leave Washington City for good. As Colonel Baker began telling me even more about the movements of the mysterious Loreta Velazquez, I felt very uncomfortable in his presence."

"I understand the sentiment."

"Drouet, how he could know of certain of my movements in striking detail and not also know that the lady villain of which he spoke sat in his very office at the same time was absolutely beyond me. The moment was surreal. I maintained my composure in his presence and resolved then and there to leave Washington City and head south as soon as I departed his office, never to return again."

"So, obviously, this was after you managed to sneak your way into the Yankee treasury?"

"That is a true statement, Drouet. And that is yet another

reason I fled Washington City quickly upon hearing my Yankee boss mention the capture of Loreta Velazquez. I did not want to have to answer for crimes of that magnitude in any country. Had Colonel Baker been able to identify me as a culprit in the treasury shenanigans I would have hung for sure.

"So, I removed myself from Baker's circle at the close of the war without putting an end to the notorious lady spy, Loreta Janeta Velazquez. I did begin tidying up that business when I arrived back in New Orleans a few weeks ago as Colonel Snider. In the taverns and other establishments frequented by blue-coats in the Vieux Carre, I began letting it be known that I, Colonel Snider, had seen to it myself that Velazquez had been eradicated in no uncertain terms. Word of it soon spread so thoroughly that I began hearing conversations of it as I passed by groups of people or sat in a public house sipping on bourbon."

"A brilliant word of mouth campaign, to be sure, Loreta. But why did you have to do her in? I'm particularly fond of her, you know."

"Loreta Velazquez needed to be put to rest, at least for the time being, at least until animosities toward me in the north quieted to a considerable degree."

"Your secrets—all of them—are safe with me."

"And yours with me, Drouet—every dark and delicious one of them."

"Okay, so please elaborate on this treasury business, as I just have to know how you charmed your way into such a high place in the land of blue-coats."

"So I told you I had a reason for mentioning Baker successfully exposing corruption across the Federal government, and for expounding on how I learned of other, up to then, unknown officials whose existence I learned from my Confederate confidants in Washington City.

"These facts will help you understand how I gained sufficient enough trust from Baker to be directed by him to help uncover more rascals within Lincoln's national treasury.

"I learned early on in the war how our Confederate agents made great use of the Federal treasury to obtain cash for their activities against our enemy. All of that had to do with utilizing Confederate sympathizers in the Federal treasury department.

"Both sides were involved in a multitude of counterfeit schemes to injure the national credit of the other, so I did not hesitate to involve myself in this game at the first opportunity afforded me. That occasion was made available to me by none other than Colonel Lafayette Baker, director of Lincoln's national detective agency.

"Baker always seemed to have a goodly horde of Confederate bills on hand to be used by his agents in the field. He had given me these bills to use on several of my own trips south while 'in his service.'

"Having gained enough confidence from Baker as to my diehard loyalty to the Federal cause, I soon felt sufficiently safe to approach a Confederate spy in the Federal treasury. I learned of this gentleman's existence from our own Confederate operatives hidden throughout Washington and New York City. Even though this Confederate sympathizer within the treasury had proven time and again to be an efficient spy for our cause, he was not the sort of man for whom I had much admiration. He exuded a weak persona, and this made working closely with him seem particularly distasteful. Nonetheless, one cannot be too picky in choosing one's associates in the undercover business, so I marched on like a soldier.

"My Confederate operative friends assured me I could approach this clerk and gain access to the private rooms of the treasury building, as this official was intimately knowledgeable as to the villainies being performed there and with the individuals working within these rooms directly involved with those traitorous practices. My Confederate associates also felt confident I could secure from the clerk a letter of introduction to one occupying a supreme position within the Federal government. Indeed, I obtained this letter, and when the name of the highly placed Federal official was named by the clerk, it caused me great astonishment.

"The clerk worded the letter of introduction in such a clever way that its reader would understand completely that I wanted to speak with him about matters of which no one else should be aware.

"I went to the office of this gentleman forthwith, presented the letter, and watched with great satisfaction as the official's face went from creamy white to beet red while his hands trembled with the rapidity of a lamb twitching its tail. Indeed, his outward countenance was such that I feared he would arouse suspicion from others in the room. It took him quite some time to regain his composure, and when he finally managed to utter actual words, they were simply commonplace utterances meant for the ears of those around us and not for mine.

"With this shaking little man, I knew I had found one so thoroughly immersed in traitorous corruption that I should own him completely if I played my cards right.

"My new jittery friend asked me to jot down my address, and then he gave me a gesture giving me to know I should leave at once, which I did. But, I left knowing I would hear from him soon and I was right, for he called on me the evening of the same day.

"I allowed him in my hotel room, and he immediately remarked that he had been making inquiries with regard to me. He said Colonel Baker had mentioned me in the highest regard, and that bit of information gave me the utmost confidence that I stood well with the secret-service chief. I felt reassured that my various ruses to take in one of Lincoln's top detectives had been working as planned.

"So, the gentleman began talking about the most unrelated of topics, seemingly making every effort not to actually say anything of any importance. He carried on about how he was not quite certain as to why I contacted him, but that he would endeavor to do anything in his power to assist me in whatever was my purpose.

"I decided to come straight to the point, plain and simple. I told him that I and my unnamed associates possessed full knowledge of the shenanigans occurring in the respective treasury bureaux and of the individuals carrying out the monkey business. I related to him that a full investigation could be initiated immediately to bring all those responsible in the tomfooleries to swift justice.

"Drouet, with that, I promise you I had his full attention. Never had I sat before as terrified a man as this one.

"But, I told him that the aforementioned tactics could be forestalled if he joined in our plan to share in the fruits of the fraudulent activities regularly transpiring in the treasury department. I communicated that I desired to have in my possession one or more of the electrotype impressions of the bond note plates used to create the counterfeit issues and that I also needed access to the printing bureau of the treasury whenever necessary to communicate with certain parties therein.

"Even though he gave me a look acknowledging that I now owned him, he nonetheless hesitated in fully committing to the plan, saying that if he cooperated with me, he was placing his life in my hands. He stated he could never sleep well at night pondering how easily I could betray him.

"I assured him that I cared not a wit about his past activities, that I needed his assistance in the current matters we had discussed, and that he would personally share in the profits of our clandestine work.

"I assured him that I was involved in this right along with him and the others in the various treasury bureaux. I could be implicated as easily as himself, and that he must surely know of my discreetness and trustworthiness in these types of matters, especially as he considered my example of stealthy work right in front of Colonel Baker.

"I will never forget his almost exact words in responding to this:

"Yes, I know your reputation for skill and secrecy, and you seem to have played it exceedingly well with Baker. I am highly pleased that somebody has managed to get it over on that fellow, as he has been making an infernal nuisance of himself around here."

We then began discussing business in a rather direct fashion.

"Delighted with our mutual consensus, my new friend agreed to furnish any capital needed to carry out our plans. He agreed to all of the necessary preliminary bribing to get the required cooperation of certain parties, and we established his percentage of the spoils.

"He then went on to explain that certain introductions would have to be made for me to begin the work of securing the fraudulent plates needed for our nefarious endeavors.

"He also surprised me by recommending that we ponder the profits to be enjoyed by extracting genuine notes and bonds and then returning them after a few rotations in the market. Of course, we also deliberated the advantages to be had by floating counterfeit Federal and Confederate bonds in certain markets at certain rates and the exact methods by which to do it.

"Before he left my hotel room, he wrote a note signed with a private mark. He told me to take this note to a certain prominent administrator at a certain bureau of the treasury connected with printing. He suggested I deliver the note on the following day.

"I took the note to the individual, and he did not appear in the least surprised to see me. This gave me to know he had been notified of my intent to visit him. He read the note at once and referred me to one of his subordinates with whom I was to meet at an appointed hour later the same day.

"This subordinate was responsible for all of the rascalities occurring in his particular bureau of the treasury, but he was not inclined to speak of any of it directly at the time. The subordinate would not agree to meet anywhere near the general public, so arrangements were made for the two of us to meet under a certain cedar tree in the eastern section of the Smithsonian Institution grounds at nine o'clock in the evening.

"I was given to know that this man and his father worked as printers in the bureau and both were responsible for defrauding the Federal government of colossal sums and for foisting upon the public immense quantities of bogus bonds and notes.

"As was my custom, I arrived earlier than the appointed time at the cedar tree, hid myself in a clump of shrubs and waited and watched lest a certain deception might attempted on me. After all, I was working to penetrate the circle of a very lucrative clandestine enterprise and perhaps some of its members determined to see me hastily eliminated from the situation in some manner or another.

"It seemed a great amount of time had elapsed before I heard footsteps and the sound of a cough made in a manner giving me knowledge my man had arrived. I stepped out of the shrubs and bade the gentleman a 'good evening.'

"He said, 'Well, I see you showed. How are you?'

"I replied that I am always punctual when it comes to my business and that punctuality is the road to wealth.

"I got down to business forthwith and proposed to him my plans to be given electrotype duplicates of bonds and currency plates such as we knew were made by certain parties within the bureaux. My new friend deemed this plan insignificant when compared with his own grandiose proposal.

"I replied that if I was to risk imprisonment for helping to carry out the scheme of another, then I should at least hear its details.

"These are as near to his exact words as I can recall from memory:

"'I have the wherewithal and desire necessary to carry out the biggest financial crime of our day, the grandest ever attempted, and I am certain we can manage it if we get started at once. You have contacted the right man with whom to participate, for no other man in Washington City has at his disposal the facilities required to carry it to fruition. I know of every man in every department, of every private entrance into every building in Washington City and of every financial high crime and misdemeanor occurring in the city at any point in time. I propose that we remove Federal money and bonds from the treasury to use for speculative designs while also floating bogus bonds upon the English market, Federal and Confederate. I will manage the assorted details on the treasury end of it; you play the middle as a go-between while our select New York and Philadelphia brokers work the outside business.'

"Well, Drouet, I stood flabbergasted and somewhat afraid of the enormity of his great design, as surely the footprints left by we criminals in the grand scheme would attract the attention of Colonel Baker and his legion of detectives. My new friend assured me that we could start out small, working our way up as we saw fit, all the while replacing the borrowed money in the treasury as it came back to us.

"So, I told him that I would accept the job as the go-between, but stipulated that he could never, ever let me be known to a third party, and that the money would have to be left in a safe spot where I could pick it up without risk of detection or else it would have to be delivered to me in person.

"He agreed, and we went to work."

"What about the electrotype plates? Did you get them?"

"My lover, those plates were my chief objective at the outset, and I never lose sight of original intentions. As soon as the profits from the scheme began rolling in, and as soon as I felt comfortable enough to pursue it, I began deploying my time and energy to the matter of the electrotype plates."

"Loreta, do you know what I like about you?"

She smiled in anticipation of my answer.

"Your fascinating story is exactly how time goes by when you and I are together—slow and easy. I like that. Please proceed with your adventurous tale."

"Well, you know that from the outset I asked about getting my hands on those plates numerous times. It was the same with my new big-scheming friend; I never allowed that he should forget my desire to secure one or more of these.

"I mentioned the matter to him on multiple occasions, but he never seemed eager to assist in making this happen.

"Then, one day, as we were about to part after a meeting in which he learned that he would soon receive a hefty payout of profits, he consented to my wishes and arranged to have a plate delivered to my room at the Kirkwood House on Pennsylvania Avenue and Twelfth Street."

Loreta's comment about having stayed in the Kirkwood House in Washington City piqued some interest on my part, so I had to interrupt.

"Isn't the Kirkwood House the home of Vice-President Andrew Johnson while in Washington City?"

"Yes, you are correct."

"Did you ever see him while staying there?"

"Yes, I did. In fact, I met with him on more than one occasion."

"I won't ask about what you discussed with him."

"You will be the first one to know about my dealings with Mr. Andrew Johnson when the time comes, I assure you."

"Enough about him for now. Tell me about that plate."

"Well, the delivered plate was used for printing one hundred dollar compound interest notes. I placed it under lock and key in my trunk immediately upon receiving it. Soon afterward, I received another plate, one used for printing fractional currency.

"Now, in New York, my associates and I began an operation with certain brokers by which we turned Federal money removed from the treasury over and over again as briskly as possible, receiving handsome returns each time. Some of the cash was invested in bogus Confederate and other securities, and these were sold to brokers for the English markets.

"The transaction sizes varied, but one banker took over sixty thousand dollars' worth, another took twenty-one thousand, and many, many others took lesser amounts. We were paid in English exchange and gold which we had converted into greenbacks forthwith.

"We engaged in a healthy business of genuine and counterfeit Federal and Confederate securities right up until Lee signed the surrender.

"Now, I know you want to hear about our work with the electrotype plates. I can tell you that the person to whom I entrusted the first plate delivered to me eighty-five thousand dollars' worth of one-hundred-dollar compound interest notes.

These bogus notes appeared identical to the genuine articles, so it was easy to have twenty-five thousand dollars' worth sent to England where we received exchange for them, with the remaining paper disposed of through banks and assorted other avenues.

"In all of this, whether dealing with actual or counterfeit paper, it seemed that the longer the war went on, the spirit of speculation increased with little regard as to the exact methods employed. The speculators included men high and low, from the most obscure to the very prominent."

Loreta mentioned some of the names of these prominent officials, but I refrain from repeating in order to protect the identities of various parties active in the K.G.C. then and perhaps even now.

"Drouet, I can tell you that we Confederates took full advantage of that prevailing cavalier spirit in matters of high finance right up until the very end. My superiors told me that if we couldn't use the returns in the war effort, then we would store it away for use later in the advancement of the cause.

"Now, Drouet, you understand why I wanted to have Loreta Janeta Velazquez disappear for a long time. If any of my associates in those matters have disclosed my involvement or ever choose to disclose my involvement, well then its prison for me."

"Loreta, were any of the ensuing profits from the treasury jobs made available for the K.G.C.?"

"Yes, and there was no other way by which these crimes could be committed without the Circle's help. Its members throughout the Federal government proved successful time and again in squelching any real prying into our wicked affairs. The K.G.C.'s coffers are swelling, thanks to the treasury department of the United States."

"Okay, Loreta, time for a sensitive question. Was Vice-President Johnson involved in making any of the aforementioned happen?"

"I said before that you would be the first to know about him when the time came, but I won't keep you in the dark about him any longer, my lover. Yes, Johnson was involved in a multitude of activities regarding my involvement with the treasury, and with so, so much more. There's something else I have to confide in you, Drouet, and it has to stay between you and me."

"If we can't trust each other then we're both in trouble. Share whatever is on your mind."

"Remember when I told you about sitting in the same room eye-to-eye with Colonel Baker as he requested that I bring in Loreta Janeta Velazquez? Well, during that same meeting, I asked him what the Federals would do with those suspected of conspiring to kill Lincoln. He responded by stating in the most certain of terms that they would all be hung, and swiftly. The reason I tell you this is because I believe Baker suspects Loreta Velazquez of being a part of that conspiracy."

"Why do you suspect this?"

"Don't ask me why. It's just a feeling. There is something else I remember from that last meeting with Baker. News had spread about the assassination of Lincoln, and I just happened to be sitting across the desk from Baker when he read a note from the secretary of war Stanton placing him in charge of finding John Wilkes Booth and the rest of those involved in the conspiracy to assassinate the president.

"He then called an aide into his office and told him to track at once down his cousin, Luther, who he often used in matters of a sensitive nature, and to get him in contact with him at once. I heard him whisper to the aide that he wanted Booth brought back to Washington City by whatever means necessary. He even mentioned the reward money as something in which he was personally interested.

"Baker's aide inquired as to the possible location of Booth, and Baker quickly responded that he most assuredly knew of the exact location of the assassin and to please get Luther in contact with him at once. Then, in a hushed tone, the aide asked Baker another question that I could not hear. Baker answered with a whisper, but I heard him say, 'The roads everywhere are covered by thousands of former Rebels on their way home. Tell Luther to bring me back a Booth!' I don't know what he meant by 'a Booth,' but the wording struck me as rather curious at the time."

"Loreta, that is more than odd I have to admit. How would Baker know where to find Booth? And wasn't it highly suspicious of Baker to send a close family relative on such a mission?"

"I don't know exactly, but history will record that he sent his cousin to the exact spot in Virginia where history records Booth had actually hidden. And, I must tell you, he only employed his cousin when there was something in it for the Bakers personally or when his cousin might have to take over the mission altogether from those originally assigned its command.

"Also, secretary of war Stanton had declared martial law in Washington City on account of the assassination, and Lafayette Baker excelled mightily in that kind of situation. He was a thug at his core and would gladly have a confession beat out of someone if not volunteered otherwise. The more martial law, the better is how Baker undoubtedly saw the situation. Anyway, something strange was amidst with Baker. Also, something that a lot of people did not know at the time is that Baker and Stanton worked closely together; in fact, they worked as a veritable team."

The bit of information concerning Baker suspecting Loreta's participation in the Lincoln assassination interested me greatly at the time, although I felt no shock upon hearing her mention it. I knew she ran in a world surrounded by those fully willing to employ such acts. I decided to act slightly disinterested and wait for Loreta to enlighten me about that subject whenever she felt it necessary if she ever would. Certain parts of her story came to interest me greatly at a later time.

"Loreta, I have to ask, in all the instances that you ran in the midst of Colonel Baker and his various staffers throughout the treasury, during all of those one-on-one meetings you had with Baker himself, did you not ever feel at least slightly fearful of your discovery?"

"A premonition told me I had Baker completely fooled. However, there was one man—a man who others around only addressed as Mr. Winslow—who worried me."

"Why is that?"

"Whenever he looked at me, I fathomed that he must know my every secret. He made me feel as if he could disclose everything about me at a moment's notice."

"How did you manage to remain collected in his presence?"

"I plowed through those occasions, telling myself each time that my mind only played tricks."

"I admire your staying power, my dear. Not too many could confidently carry out their duties around one such as that, and all while working in the lion's den that is Washington City. You were surrounded everywhere by those who would easily kill you had they known of your transgressions."

I knew Loreta had divulged more to me at that point and time than she would have to any other person on the planet, so I told her to save any other details for later, perhaps over a glass of Sazerac at the Pickwick.

"Now, Drouet, maybe you will enlighten me as to your adventures since we departed after the mint heist so long ago."

"Well, I cannot say that I possess the same skills as you in carrying out the charges of the K.G.C. and, by extension, for the late Confederacy. You have perfected your abilities to disguise and to deceive into an art—just more reasons that I adore you. But I, as you know from the great mint heist we carried out right here in this very city, prefer more direct approaches.

"If there is treasure in a mint building, rob it. If there are valuables in a Yankee wagon train, loot it. If there are goods needed by the Confederacy on a Yankee steamboat, raid it. And if there is gold and currency within a safe on a Yankee railroad car charging down the tracks from Cincinnati, first derail it, and then take the booty at gunpoint."

"Oh, Drouet, I do love you, and I'm glad we're back together, and in New Orleans!"

"That's good, because we have work to do, and it involves getting rid of thugs belonging to the same secret organization employing our own talents for these many years. Have you been by your home since you returned?"

"Yes, and it had been ransacked, probably by those who somehow know about our work in the mint building. They were looking for loot or at least for clues as to its whereabouts."

"I agree. Both of Father's properties, now mine, were also gone through, and I'm sure by the same people, which is why I have been living here disguised in this brothel. While I am not necessarily averse to the company here, I don't like hiding out, and I am ready to put an end to it. Plus, I don't want to take much more advantage of Maggie's good nature and hospitality."

"How do you propose to do it?"

"In direct fashion. If certain parties possess an interest in finding us, then I say let's allow them to do it when we are ready. I have a plan regarding that—but in due course."

11

NEW K.G.C. ASSIGNMENTS

I strode into the Pickwick for a much-needed Sazerac. I hadn't imbibed a fourth of the glass before a staff member of the Pickwick—a friend of mine since childhood who knew my identity despite the disguise because of the handwritten note I gave him—presented me with a sealed package roughly six inches thick. I knew the contents outlined upcoming assigned duties for yours truly on behalf of the illustrious K.G.C.

I held the heavy package and pondered the contents. What lay in store for me if I chose to follow the dictates as outlined within the ponderous tome?

The Circle had been on my mind a lot during those days. With the Confederacy having lost its bid for independence, the clandestine society had lost its reason for existence in my opinion. Further, Loreta had received word from several within her vast network of contacts that many of the society's founding members had departed the country never to return. We learned of said exoduses very soon after the war, but we only learned of the details surrounding the escapes and departures sometime later.

Using several aliases and outfitting himself in the adornments of, firstly, a French traveler, and, secondly, a humble farmer, Judah Benjamin escaped through Florida. After a perilous journey through that state, evading detection by nearby prowling Yankees more than once, he managed to reach Sarasota Bay where he boarded a friendly ship bound for the Bimini Islands. The journey across the waters proved equally dangerous for the former Confederate Secretary of State when the Union Navy detained the vessel on two different occasions. By that time, however, Benjamin had thrown away his farmer's disguise and had adorned himself in the attire of a ship's cook, replete with a stained apron and grease-smeared face.

Benjamin made his way to England where he went to work for a London newspaper while studying English Law on the side, a pursuit that led to his eventual service as Counsel to the Queen.

John Slidell, who found himself in Paris, France at the time of Lee's surrender, decided to stay there. There, one daughter married a French nobleman, Comte de St. Roman, and another married Baron Frederick Emile Erlanger, a prominent banker who had previously backed a loan to the Confederacy in the amount of $15 million.

Even though top Yankee intelligence officials suspected General Pike complicit in the assassination of Abraham Lincoln, the K.G.C. mastermind disappeared from Indian Territory and Arkansas altogether after the war. Pike made a beeline straight to Canada where he hid for a short time before eventually entering the cat's lair in Washington City. There, he won a pardon from fellow Mason and, according to many in Loreta's network, K.G.C. member, President Andrew Johnson. Our sources confirmed that President Johnson pardoned Pike one day and then met with him in the White House on the next. Upon first hearing of Johnson's K.G.C. sympathies, I stood in some disbelief, but later information convinced me that the seventeenth president of the United States had, in fact, performed certain monumental tasks in the service of The Circle.

Trust that I will elaborate on these details later in the narrative.

Once in Washington City, and after his pardon, General Pike engaged himself wholeheartedly in the minutiae of Freemasonry and did not push his luck any further with involvement in the K.G.C. as far as anyone in our network could ascertain.

While enough of the K.G.C. apparatus lived on to relay dispatches to me at the Pickwick Club, I sensed that the abandonment of the society by such prominent former leaders allowed for an immense lack of control and direction within the association, a void on which I deliberated greatly.

I finished my glass of Sazerac, ordered another, and then proceeded upstairs to a private room where I could examine the package's contents without interruption.

Once placed upon the table, the stack of paper immediately indicated an enormity of work ahead for me. I beheld a stack of checks from the Bank of Montreal in Canada, multiple smaller sealed packages intended for delivery to agents in the field without opening beforehand. I viewed page after page detailing such items as aliases used by said agents and where to find them. Their locations stretched all across the country, from Arkansas and Indian Territory to New Mexico and Colorado. The Circle tasked me with traveling to these locations when the time came to deliver these packages and checks; with visiting some of these gentlemen more than once over a period of years, paying them in increments so as to keep them quiet for as long as possible. This method allowed recollections of old events to wither away with the mild and melting influence of time; and with obtaining from these agents where they might relocate between visits.

I liked none of it.

Yours truly had traveled enough in service to the K.G.C., an organization that, with each passing day, seemed to grow more obsolete with its stated goals of forming a circle of slave-holding states, territories and countries—a truly grandiose target before the war and certainly a dubious one after it.

Now, it seemed to me, the remaining K.G.C. members who owned even half a brain were involved in a game one might call "every man for himself." With their cause lost, agents wanted payment for banks robbed, trains looted and assassinations carried out, and their overlords wanted them paid in full so as to keep their mouths shut. My job as a K.G.C. agent, and now as courier, involved making all of the above happen without incident. I also had to avoid falling into the hands of any lower level thugs aware that I alone knew the whereabouts of the mint booty. To clean up that remaining mess required baiting the hook for the fish, with me as bait, a scenario to which I did not look forward.

Without determining my next major move, I gathered the assorted ephemera, placed it back inside the larger package, enjoyed another glass of Sazerac, and made my way using a roundabout route to my room at Maggie's.

While walking through the Vieux Carre en route to Maggie's, I happened upon a lively scene on St. Ann Street. Voudou queen Marie Laveau, Father's old friend, and friend to many in New Orleans sat next to her daughter watching a large group of her followers, which included a number of recently freed slaves, dancing in the street. The animated scene of merriment attracted a large audience, myself included.

Some called Laveau a she-devil and trembled at the mention of her name, but many in New Orleans welcomed her into their homes for her abilities not only to dress hair but to tell fortunes, to craft charms, to cast spells, and to heal.

Both Father and I knew that Laveau's Voudou consisted of African traditions, Haitian Voudou, European magic, and folk Catholicism. I had visited her home on St. Ann Street in my youth and remember an altar there covered with a statue of St. Anthony and various images on paper of other saints. Laveau called on St. Anthony of Padua to help find lost articles and even to retrieve stray lovers. She sometimes called on St. Peter to open the door to the spirit world, to remove obstacles to success, to invite patrons into one's place of business and to help guard the home against trespassers.

At the back of her home, she delved into what many considered the darker elements of her faith. She had an altar for "bad work," which included such functions as preparing charms to kill, to break up love affairs and to foster chaos. That back-room altar took up the width of the room and featured candles, paper flowers and plaster statues of bears, lions, and tigers, totems of the energies she needed and sought.

Each year, on the night of June 23, two days after the summer solstice, when the human world and the spirit world connect as one, Laveau and her Voudou followers celebrated St. John's Eve on the banks of Lake Pontchartrain. The celebration had been introduced to New Orleans by both French and Spanish colonists many, many years before. Somewhere along the way, people of African descent adopted the date on which to perform their particular observances, rituals that comprised singing, dancing, sacrifices, bathing, dining, and, according to some, other less restrained pleasures. I can certainly attest that as many whites as Africans attended the yearly festivities on

June 23 as well as the other Voudou functions throughout the year.

Laveau had aged to a woman of elder years, and her eyesight had deteriorated to a state of near blindness by war's end, so I stood shocked at what happened when I ambled by in disguise near the gala on St. Ann Street that day. Even as an old woman, she reigned as a statuesque beauty with her alluring eyes, with her hair dark as night, and with her buttery gold skin – all featured aristocratically underneath a colorful seven-knotted tignon masterfully tied atop her crown. It had been some years since I had last seen her, so I couldn't help but glance her way as I strode by.

Two feet near her, with the sound of happiness and amusement all around, she stood at once, arranged herself in front of me, gazed deeply into my eyes, and spoke piercingly and decisively.

"I know things about you!"

Her daughter rose and gently took hold of Marie's arm.

"Mother, you have never seen this man."

"Is this not Broussard's son?"

"Mother, this is not him. This man does not look like Drouet at all."

"It is! I feel him nearby."

I placed my arms around the shoulders of both Laveau women and motioned them away from earshot of the crowd.

"Yes, it is me, Drouet. I am in disguise as I do not wish to be discovered by certain people right now."

The face of Marie's daughter showed amazement and disbelief, perhaps at my disguise, perhaps at her mother's ability to discern my nearness, but probably at both.

"I see more than people think I can see without good eyes, and I knew you were nearby. I knew it, I felt it. I always could feel when your father was near, too. You have grown to a man since I last saw you, but I can tell by your eyes that you are a lot like him."

"I know that you and Father were friends, and I remember visiting your home a long time ago. And, yes, I am a lot like Father was, the good with the bad, I'm afraid."

"You're honest like your father was. He came around often to the orgies years ago. Until he met Marguerite. I introduced him to her, you know. Your father loved the quadroon and octaroon ladies, preferred them over any other, and he attended many of my parties where he had all he wanted."

"I know this. Like you say, until he met Marguerite. She became his queen."

"Yes. You know, my daughter here holds the parties now, and you are welcome always. But that is not why I wanted to talk with you."

"I am always at your service, as was Father."

"You see the shadow people, don't you?"

"Yes, I do all the time. How do you know this?"

"I know many things. But, you just *see* the shadow people. I *talk* with the shadow people."

"What do they say?"

"They tell me a lot of things. They tell me death is searching for you."

"How so?"

"It is upon you with the people who seek to control you. They have death in their eyes, and you must kill them before they kill you. Deep down, you already know this."

"Yes, this is true."

"I want you to wait here."

Laveau then went inside her home and remained for perhaps thirty minutes. When she returned, she carried with her a long strip of leather holding a small leather pouch which she presented to me.

"This is your gris-gris. I give this to you for protection. Never mind what is inside the bag. Just wear it at all times. Do this for yourself, and for me."

"I will wear the gris-gris, always, and I will get to work as you say. When I am done, I will call on you again."

"It will be a happy day."

I stayed with the Laveau ladies for a while longer, enjoying the dancing and the merriment all around as we discussed Father and the wild days of old. Then, I made my way at once to Maggie's.

I figured the men I had to face were of the alleyway ilk as before—throat slashers and backstabbers, gut robbers and women killers, low-level hoodlums too simple to understand the growing insignificance of The Circle. Fine with me, I thought. I cut my teeth on just that kind of play. I told Laveau I planned on getting to work at once, and this I determined to do.

Once back at my room at Maggie's, I removed my disguise, never to use it again, and waited for Loreta who had worked hard keeping her presence unknown for the most part while back in New Orleans. We had spent most every waking hour together at Maggie's, either in my room or in the poker room honing our skills as card cheats, sending one of the girls out when we needed something instead of venturing out and attracting attention.

Loreta returned in due course, looking every bit the devious Spanish aristocrat who had won my heart with her poised and well-proportioned beauty and alluring dark charms.

"Loreta, it's time we ended this damned charade."

"Meaning?"

"Meaning, my dear, that I've tarried for too long in confronting the reasons keeping us confined to this house of melodious moans and late-night gaiety, and I'm ashamed of myself for not addressing said matters sooner."

"I know where you are heading with this. When do we start?"

"We start tonight, first at our place in the Quarter, then at Father's old place, and finally at your home."

"I see you are out of that silly disguise."

"Yes, and for good. From now on, you and I remain arm-in-arm, and we show ourselves as often as possible all over town. Anyone on the prowl for us should soon fathom we are here for the taking, but we will stand at the ready when they attempt to make that happen."

"I love being with you, Drouet."

"You could choose far superior company, I'm sure. Please explain this hold I have on such a stately beauty as the great Loreta Janeta Velazquez."

"Well, you are rarely boring, and never for long at that."

"That's a compliment?"

She answered with a sly laugh.

"Darling, I hope you're carrying your little pocket cannon."

Loreta stood, walked to within arms-length of me, extended her right leg forward and began rolling up the Crepe of the Rococo dress to reveal not only the shapely curves underneath but also the .44-caliber Henry derringer tucked snuggly within the high lace garter.

Incidentally, it struck me as interesting at the time that she carried the exact same derringer used by Booth to assassinate Lincoln, but I thought nothing further of it as she slid her dress back down to conceal the firearm once again. I fully knew that Loreta continued to live by her own devices within a vast network of spies, informants, cutthroats and gullible suitors with whom she kept constant contact and that she possessed immense knowledge concerning the K.G.C. and of the late war far beyond anything I might imagine.

But, none of this bothered me a whit. I found her interesting and enjoyed her company immensely over any other lady I knew.

"Loreta, I never tire of handling difficult matters with you. Now, do prepare yourself for a night of rather dark business. I shall return directly, and we will commence when the sun sets. I have business at the Pickwick.

I met my K.G.C. contact at the Pickwick and began setting matters straight at once.

"I have thoroughly gone over all the contents of the package. I have the names, the aliases, their locations, the amounts owed them and the dates on which they should be paid. But there is one thing I need to make perfectly clear. I will not travel across the continent performing this commitment. When agents require compensation, when they require receipt of certain important information to remain undercover and out of sight of the government in Washington City now, and in the coming years, then they will come to New Orleans and find me here at the Pickwick. They will prove their K.G.C. bonafides as required, and I will fulfill my duties as pledged to General Pike so long ago."

The last item we discussed concerned the booty from the mint heist. He gave direction from on high as to how to divvy those proceeds and when. He then asked where I had hidden the stash, and I refused to say. I had anticipated the question and stood ready with my answer.

My contact asked that I write all of that down on paper and I did so. He pledged to hand the letter to his contact and so begin its track up the ladder to higher K.G.C. leaders, whoever they were. Of their names, I knew not, and held no concern for them, regardless.

Lower level K.G.C. thugs still roaming the streets of New Orleans concerned me more, and I had grown tired of hiding from them. I needed to have them in front of me so as to confront them head-on and straightaway, with making myself readily available to said cutthroats the fastest way to make that happen. I had resolved to walk the streets of New Orleans without disguise, without shying from anyone, and if confronted by those planning to beat out of me the location of the mint booty then so be it, all the better in facilitating the necessary clean up.

On my way back to Loreta, I made sure to amble up and down more streets of the Vieux Carre than necessary—better for everyone to know that Drouet Broussard had survived the war and had returned home. My presence served as the "open for business" sign for anyone desiring a personal meeting.

Once back at Maggie's I gathered a few belongings, locked arms with Loreta, and then we made our way to the residence in the Vieux Carre where we planned to serve as honey for any K.G.C. bees roaming thereabouts. We engaged in a dangerous business to be sure, but an enterprise altogether necessary for making the streets of the Crescent City safe for us again.

The first few days and nights proved uneventful toward that goal. After growing bored waiting for something to happen at the apartment, we decided to spend more time at the Pick-wick drinking Sazeracs, playing poker and conversing late into the night. As it became clearer to both of us that we lived in the last days of any real K.G.C. influence, we both began talking a bit more freely to one another about previous work with the clandestine group.

I made it known to her that I never retrieved any of the plunder from the mint building after I stashed it away so many years before. She often asked about the cache's location, but I danced around the answer. All in good time, I told her. Loreta danced around details in a similar way when asked if she played a role in the Lincoln assassination, but she did go so far as to say I would certainly ascertain more of that story on my own in my continued but reluctant role as K.G.C. agent in New Orleans in the coming years.

"Just know that you will one day fathom all of the details of that affair, Drouet, and you will still love me."

"Of that I am certain. Far be it for me to question any of your devices in the line of duty during the late melee."

"What you are trying very hard to say without being offensive is that we are both rogues drawn to treachery and quick to violence, you in your way and me in mine."

"Yes, we are both made of the same cloth. But, don't think for a moment that I hold any of it against you. "

"Not for a minute. I know that run-of-the-mill fair ladies hold no charm with you. With you, I've only to worry about those quadroon beauties you and your late father always fancied."

"I don't deny any of that, but you've nothing of which to worry, Loreta. You own the full width and breadth of my affections."

One observation made during her wartime work that Loreta made no qualms in divulging centered around the K.G.C. leadership.

"Call it women's intuition, Drouet, but there were many times during the last four years when I got the feeling that Pike, Slidell, Benjamin, and Bickley were not the ultimate authorities in matters concerning The Circle. It comes down to the way certain things were said, to certain things I saw. I believe certain forces outside the country reigned over the apparatus that is slowly crumbling before our eyes."

"I agree. It sure seems that many of our former overlords are finding favor and safe harbor in the friendly confines of Europe as we speak. Is that what you are getting at?"

"That's exactly what I'm getting at. Benjamin is more than friendly with certain European bankers, having entertained some of them in this very club before the war started. The same with Slidell."

"Maybe all of our recent woes were exacerbated by foreign interests, powers that needed a country split in half and at war with itself. Maybe Lincoln achieved a great feat in keeping it all together against powerful European trifling."

"I heard much the same kind of speculation from some of my northern contacts while in the employ of Baker. We may never know."

"It's all behind us now. Let's enjoy life, you and me. I plan on only casually fulfilling my remaining duties with the K.G.C., and that's only because I made a promise to a certain Confederate general who commanded my friends during that late struggle."

"Drouet, for all practical purposes, he has washed his hands of The Circle, or at least that's what I'm hearing from my network. He's working to find favor with the new government in Washington City and to make his mark on his first and real love, Scottish Rite Freemasonry. You shall never see him or hear from him again."

12

UNFINISHED BUSINESS

With disguises finally discarded, many were the suspicious glances aimed at Loreta and me as we walked the streets of the Vieux Carre, as we dined in the evening and as we played poker and faro with the gaming crowd on the riverboats and at any number of New Orleans' gambling establishments until the early morning hours.

One night at Tujague's, in the charming company of Loreta, we enjoyed delicious servings of spicy shrimp smoldered with a piquant remoulade sauce and glasses of Sazerac. As the hours of enjoying fine food, drink and conversation passed, a sense of foreboding enveloped me.

Despite the pleasant evening, I could not help but notice shadow people lurking about in the corners.

I settled with Guilliaume, the proprietor, and spoke my adieus, but not before asking him to watch over Loreta as I stepped out to reconnoiter the cobblestone thoroughfares, recessed doorways and dark alleyways along Decatur and the nearby thoroughfares of Madison, Chartres, and Dumaine. Before heading back toward Tujague's, I decided to walk about halfway down to the river and look over the area. After standing motionless for several minutes to ascertain any unusual movement or sound, and detecting nothing, I turned and began walking back toward Tujague's.

Just then, a dark silhouette emerged from behind a live oak and ran pell-mell straight in the direction of one Drouet Broussard, transforming a perfectly serene moment to one of impending death. The silhouette's grunts and heavy breathing drew ever closer, and I fathomed at once that the time lay upon me.

As I whirled to confront my pursuer, I glimpsed the shine of steel coming my way in the moonlight. The blade's owner came at my arm as if to maim, but not fancying loss of limb, I pulled my right-side Bowie and slashed to kill, going for the gullet and taking down the dark figure with only two thrusts, in low and up fast. The gurgling heap lay there dying as I made straightaway for Tujague's and Loreta.

In the safety of the apartment, I related to Loreta my close call with the assailant, both of us now fully understanding the vigilance necessary for our continued longevity.

The weeks passed with no lively event, and I guessed the number of my enemies had possibly thinned down to single digits, but I remained ever watchful of possible assailants lurking in the darkness. I refused to fall into a false sense of security until I knew for certain that the streets of the Crescent City were safe for Loreta and myself once again.

One moonless night on our balcony in the Vieux Carre while watching the lively street below, Loreta suggested making the short walk to Bourbon Street for an absinthe frappe at Aleix's Coffee House, an establishment actually more of a public house than the name implied. Regarding her proposition as a model idea, I agreed, donned my hat and cape, and we departed straightaway.

We sought to attract as little attention as possible on each of our jaunts, with such the case on this night as we passed through the streets and near the dark alleyways. While the usual spirit of gaiety filled the streets, it did not go unnoticed the occasional interested glimpse or the sideways peek trained our way while en route.

We arrived at the two-hundred block of Bourbon Street and began making merry at once with a familiar server and a few friendly faces at the tables. We spent a few hours in the confines of the establishment before deciding the happy night must end. As had grown my custom during those perilous days before leaving an establishment, especially at night, I asked Loreta to remain at the table while I patrolled the immediate environs outside the front door.

As soon as I reached the already opened front doorway, I heard whispering voices outside before ever stepping out onto Bourbon Street.

"You're sure he's in there, and you're sure it's Broussard?"

"My eyes don't lie. And he's with his lady friend."

"All the better. I have questions of both of them that could make us rich. We crack both of their skulls when they come out. Don't kill 'em, understand?"

"I know."

Their voices indicated that both men stood to the left side of the door as I faced it from within. I returned to the table and apprised Loreta of the state of affairs.

"What shall we do, Drouet?"

"I'm not immediately sure, but I grow tired of slashing men in the darkness."

"Yes, I can understand your sentiment in that regard."

Loreta pondered intently for just a few seconds before uttering the most ingenious solution to the night's singular predicament.

"If you could dispose of both men for years without killing them and without either of them knowing you did it would you be interested? Because if you are, I have a solution over on Gallatin Street."

The mention of Gallatin Street raised my interest, to be sure. I knew the locality for its streets dimly lit, for its dark streets slippery and wet, for its alleyways dark and dank, for its window shutters battered and broken, and for long rows of tall houses showcasing windows with nothing but darkness behind.

I knew firsthand of the tremendous concentration of carnage and sin within its cheap boarding houses, raucous dance halls, wild bawdy houses, and groggeries altogether too seedy to garner the title of saloon—and all of this packed together on the wharf where seamen from every corner of the globe lurked in the shadows.

Located between Ursulines and Barracks streets between the river and Decatur, the locale offered a high probability of death for anyone willing to risk the pleasures of its environs. Many a man, both rough and polished, had entered its private rooms with the ladies of Gallatin Street and were never seen again this side of the veil, and many were the dapper gentlemen who had entered the surroundings walking upright only to receive a knock in the head before ending up sold for ten dollars on the river to any number of ship's captains needing able-bodied sailors.

Quite simply, to enter Gallatin Street after dark in those days meant placing one's life at risk.

"Loreta, pray, what devices does that mind of yours conjure up on this night?"

"Do you trust me?"

"I was about to say 'yes, with some hesitation,' but I reverse myself. I trust you with my life."

I then bowed.

"Well, you may regret that reversal before the night is over."

"I'm all in. The story is not a conventional one, yours and mine, so what plan have you?"

Loreta then revealed to me her idea, a design cold, hard, brutal and cunning, and one I admired as could only come from her on such short notice.

She then departed to the kitchen where she conversed for a short time with our friend the proprietor. Soon, she returned to our table with two short-handled cast-iron skillets. I took them both. From there, she departed quickly back to the kitchen, retrieved a few more items there and then began her ascent up the stairs to the second floor of the coffee house.

I arose from the table and made my way to near the front door and the two saboteurs awaiting outside. Staying within the confines of the coffee house, but ever near the front door, I awaited my signal.

Maybe two minutes ticked by before Loreta had made her way up the stairs and into the second-floor room immediately over the spot of our two greeters-to-be. Without hesitation, she opened the door to the front balcony from which she dropped an assortment of pots and pans to the cobblestone walkway below. I rushed out the door at once and found our would-be assailants with both their backs to me as they attempted to understand the nearby commotion to their left. That was the scenario I desired to see, as it made coming up behind both men and clobbering their heads in with the cast-iron skillets an act all the easier to perform.

Both men crumpled instantaneously across the cobble-stones. I grabbed both men by their collar and drug them to the rear of the establishment. By the time I had hauled the bodies back, Loreta had descended the stairs, ran to the rear of the building and directed us to a horse provided by the proprietor. We draped both men harum-scarum over the back of the horse and proceeded down an alleyway and away from the scene as rapidly as possible. In no time, we found ourselves several blocks away and ever closer to Gallatin Street.

Once, emerging from a dark alleyway, one of the hoodlums slid off the horse and fell to the street. Luckily, no passersby noticed our presence and I hoisted the cargo back atop the steed.

"Drouet, it's imperative these men remain unconscious. If either one of them makes a move then give his head another knock."

"I may have you do it."

Using devious routes 'round and about, our merry band made its way through the dark streets and alleyways first across the thoroughfares of Royal, Chartres, and Decatur, and then over the ways of Bienville, Conti, St. Louis, Toulouse and St. Peter until we arrived in the vicinity of Gallatin Street.

Ambling slowly so as avoid attention, we made our way past tall shuttered houses with broken windows, by dimly-lit or completely darkened establishments emitting yells, curses, and screams from within.

We brought the steed to a halt so as to better arrange the cargo when a drunken sailor bedecked in a blue sailor shirt and cap emerged from a nearby haunt, grunted, and then pointed back in the direction from whence he came.

"Ay! If it's fun and frolickin' yer seekin' then sail right on in there! They can handle you one at a time or both together, whatever your pleasure."

In order to rid ourselves of the observer, and to perhaps keep him quiet as to our presence, I considered it prudent to toss him a gold coin from out of my pocket.

"There, go back and frolic the rest of the night away, but be gone and stay quiet. Do we understand one another?"

"Bless you for a gentleman, sir! I am gone, and I am quiet, as quiet as the shadows."

The drunken sailor then returned back into the dive from whence he came.

"Which of these illustrious establishments is our destination tonight, Loreta?"

"To the Amsterdam House to see someone friendly to the late cause, someone I learned about from within the K.G.C. web—the owner of the den, Dan O'Neil."

"I've heard of him, a dangerous man. Can we trust him?"

"We can trust him with what we need tonight, to be sure."

When finally we arrived at the front of the Amsterdam House, Loreta began making her way to the entrance but stopped short and turned back to me.

"If either of our friends atop that horse makes the slightest move then do what is necessary to return them to sleep. I shall return in short order."

No more than ten minutes had elapsed when Loreta returned with the proprietor of the esteemed enterprise, Dan O'Neil. A strapping hulk of a figure standing over six-and-a-half feet and appearing well over the two-hundred-and-fifty-pound mark, O'Neil owned a reputation as a tough customer who resorted to ruthlessness whenever necessary. He owned and managed a guzzle-house where men drank themselves into a state brave enough to dally with any one of his stable of willing ladies in the upstairs parlors, environs where some men entered never to emerge again. No doubt, many were knocked over the head and thrown aboard the various vessels of sea captains who frequented the groggery.

In spite of the known crimes committed regularly in the den, no one ever asked questions of Dan O'Neil—not the police, not the city leaders, not the occupying Yankees. Others before them had crossed the goonish devil, but none from those aforementioned ranks desired to join that fraternal order of the now deceased.

O'Neil walked out to inspect the cargo but sized me up first.

"Heard of you. You're Broussard the slasher. You do good work, thorough-like, and then you disappear, and no one is the wiser—except for me. I know what goes on. It's my business to know. If ever I could use a refined New Orleans couple in my apparatus it would certainly be you two."

O'Neil then walked up beside our cargo, using the hair mops of both men as handles to raise their heads for facial inspections.

"These will do. Don't tell me where you obtained 'em because I don't want to know. What's your askin' price?"

Loreta answered at once.

"Ten dollars apiece."

Neither of us needed the money, but Loreta refused to insult the gangster by refusing his payment. We both knew O'Neil and his type. The criminal might toss a man from an upstairs parlor window out onto the stone pathways below and not think twice about it ever again, but he paid his debts, and pity the man who looked upon him as a low-life charity case.

"I'd gladly pay you twenty each for these strappin' bucks, but I'll see your askin' price and gladly so. Broussard, if you hoist the one up, then I'll hoist the other."

With that, O'Neil and I took the men to a back room within his groggery and laid them out behind a locked iron door with an armed guard on the other side.

"Slasher, by this time tomorrow, both those men will be out upon the gulf waters helpin' an appreciative ship's captain."

"The longer they're gone, the better. I considered opening them both up like the others you mentioned, but a man can develop habits."

"Aye, you're ever the gentleman, even in the bloody line of work that you are. I don't understand it, but any friend of Miss Velazquez is a friend of mine. She's helped me out more than once in our mutual line of work, and I'll leave it at that."

"Then may I ask a favor?"

O'Neil nodded in the affirmative.

"As I said, I could have killed these two men here and never had worry of them again around a sinister corner or lurking in the shadows for me. I need them gone for a goodly number of years, and they must not know who sold them out to the high seas."

"That's all? Of course, but that's askin' no favor at all. As for the part about who sold 'em to me, just know we keeps our mouths shut on Gallatin Street. And as for the latter, I've been placin' poor bastards such as them on ships for many a year, and I've never seen a one of 'em ever again."

"I'm indebted to you, O'Neil, and count you as a friend."

"Not a bit indebted to me you are. It's been my pleasure and a gentleman you are for sure no doubt. You're welcome at the Amsterdam any time with your pick of any of my ladies with no trouble."

"Thank you, and I will remember your generosity."

We shook hands, and then Loreta and I departed Gallatin Street at a steady, careful and watchful clip through the ghostly, wet streets and murky alleyways toward home.

Our Shanghai deal with O'Neil was the first and last time I ever sold another human being into an arrangement with which they did not agree, but I justified the act as far better for the two than winding up laid wide open in a back alley of the Vieux Carre never to see the sun or moon again. While my family had never involved itself directly in the institution of slavery, I allowed that I had now participated directly in an institution somewhat akin to it—the custom of impressment.

Regardless, the incident began receding from the forefront of my mind as the celebration of Mardi Gras grew nearer. Everywhere people prepared for the coming merriment, for a Fat Tuesday that had not been celebrated in New Orleans since before the outbreak of the late war. A few years before that great conflict ensued, in 1857, Father had teamed with his friends Albert Pike, Judah Benjamin, John Slidell and others in the newly-formed Mystic Krewe of Comus, the first secret carnival society, to elevate Mardi Gras from an unorganized festival to a spectacle of beauty complete with torchlit processions, ostentatious floats, marching bands, colorful costumes and extravagant balls.

I will always remember that first night of revelry as organized by the Krewe back in 1857. The Krewe made its debut on the streets of New Orleans at nine o'clock in the evening on February twenty-fourth of that year. The Krewe called upon Mayor Charles Waterman and announced itself before marching through the streets while bedecked in dazzling costumes and carrying glaring torchlights en route to the theatre where awaited a spectacular gathering of elegance and style. Four connected tableaux featuring over one-hundred characters from Milton's *Paradise Lost* served as the barrier threshold to the ballroom. Barriers then removed, a magnificent ball commenced in which the invitees of the Mystic Krewe of Comus participated. At the stroke of midnight, members of the Mystic Krewe silently departed the premises, allowing their friends and guests to make merry all through the night until the "coming of the gray morn."

The following year, the Krewe assembled in Lafayette Square where they "kidnapped" the good Mayor Waterman before proceeding through the streets where thousands of excited revelers greeted Comus, Momus, Janus, Flora, Diana, Jupiter and a host of other deities of old showcased in splendid procession. At the theatre, four tableaux were presented, and a great dance commenced as before. Terpsichore, the goddess of music, song, and dance, received her crown as queen of the night, and then the members of the Mystic Krewe of Comus silently departed the theatre allowing their special invitees to delight in mischief and merrymaking throughout the long hours of the night.

Subsequent Mardi Gras proved equal, if not superior in mystery and magnificence up until the year 1861, the last Fat Tuesday celebration before the firing on Fort Sumter.

So, we found ourselves in the year 1866, and word spread throughout the streets of the Crescent City that the Mystic Krewe of Comus planned to walk again as before, exciting in revelers many pleasant memories of the past. Cards passed around portrayed imagery representing the four gloomy and uninteresting years of the war since the last parade. The spirit of merriment ran supreme once again as men, women, and children planned for the calling of the Mayor, the procession to the theatre, and for the four tableaux representing the themes for the year 1866—"The Past," "The Present," "The Future," and "The Court of Comus."

The great night came, and throngs of revelers lined the streets to behold the magnificence and pomp of Comus marching once again.

Carrying blazing torchlights with which to illuminate the night, Comus emerged from its den on Tchoupitoulas Street between Lafayette and Girod streets at around nine o'clock. The over one-hundred-member procession made its way along the banking district of Magazine Street and by the handsome townhouses of Camp Street. It passed Julia Row and the "Thirteen Sisters" that were thirteen brick townhouses considered amongst the finest addresses in the Crescent City.

Comus marched along the part of St. Charles Avenue

between Lafayette Square and Tivoli Place before eventually crossing Poydras Street. From there, the procession passed the St. Charles Theater and Academy of Music.

Sometime after ten o'clock, Comus reached the Gaiety-Variete Theater located between Carondelet and Baronne Streets, the location of the long-awaited ball.

Awaiting the colorful and brilliant procession were many notables of New Orleans, the carefully-selected recipients of the most sought-after invitation of the year who stood in awe as Comus entered the Gaiety-Variete Theater to enact its tableaux upon the opulently decorated stage.

Each of the attendees were ladies and gentlemen dressed in a high style befitting their rank and stature, a multi-hued palette of duelists and debutantes, merchants and musicians, actors and adventurers, swindlers and scoundrels, carousers and old crows, scattered throughout with secret lovers and socialites, all ornamented in brilliant masquerade masks and armed with easy talk and laughter complemented by the free flow of the highest quality of liquid spirits New Orleans could provide.

I knew the identities of most everyone in attendance regardless of their masquerade masks. In those early days, the Mystic Krewe of Comus, the Pickwick Club, and The Circle were nearly one and the same as manifested in the Crescent City. Membership of the three societies offered a veritable Who's Who of notables visiting our household during my youth. I eventually learned Father got into anything worth getting into in those days, a fact placing me directly into certain clandestine activities that now risked certain dire outcomes for me after his death. As for Father's membership in The Circle, I accepted that his involvement originated more out of social expectation than out of any strong adherence to the order's political aims.

Soon, spirits began flowing, and dancing commenced, and the great ball proceeded apace in becoming a most colorful, flirtatious and memorable spectacle. Playful discussion began with vivacious ladies present, both young and old.

Loreta looked stunning in her red evening dress hanging low enough on the shoulders to drive most men mad and other women green with jealousy. Her long, dangling, diamond-and-ruby-encrusted earrings served as the *pièce de résistance.*

She and I tested our dancing shoes together for several dances before the night took on a life of its own. While dancing, I noticed an unusual ring on her right hand and a never before seen fan held in her left. The ring showcased a large stone that capped what unmistakably appeared as a hollowed rectangle beneath. A close inspection of the fan revealed razor-sharp metal points camouflaged amidst the brilliantly colored feathers and gemstones.

Clutching her tightly as we danced, I felt of the ring and gave a close look at her fan before casting an expression her way that made known my genuine curiosity.

"Pray, Loreta, what are these little treasures on your delicate hands? I've never seen you with them before."

"The ring encases poison powder, and the fan features deadly sharpened metal prongs. Both are made for killing. The little derringer beneath my dress performs the same function but with an unfortunate loud report."

"Why the secretive weaponry at the ball tonight? Is something worrying you?"

"Let's just say that a few days ago near Jackson Square, I spied a face from afar that looked familiar."

"Of whom did the faraway countenance remind you?"

"Of someone in Colonel Baker's detective agency."

"Is that person here tonight?"

"Drouet, you and I know that no one from that world

would be invited here tonight, but something tells me it's better to be safe than sorry."

"This is true, and all the more reason for you to showcase yourself, have fun and not injure or kill any of the guests present here tonight."

I smiled as first one gentleman, and then another whisked Loreta onto the floor for dance and engaging conversation. Her admirers that night saw the same qualities in her that I always did—inviting charm and a sense of aristocracy to complement the beauty of a refined Spanish goddess. They did not know of her daring, of her intelligence, of her cunning, or of her coldness when working single-mindedly toward achieving a goal once established.

She whirled this way and that around the floor, and I occasionally caught a word or two of conversation as she passed close by. When I heard her utter the words "John St. Helen" on one such pass-by, my mind began working diligently to remember where I had heard the name before.

Soon, the images in my mind beckoned me back to my last time in Indian Territory, to a moment outside the tent of General Stand Watie some months after the end of the war. I remembered the handsome, limping gentleman with the piercing eyes and all too easy recollections from Shakespeare who announced himself as John St. Helen.

I filed that knowledge away for easy retrieval later when at once I spied the beautiful widow St. Croix, resplendent behind her brilliant, glittering mask and underneath the latest hairstyle from Paris, a sort of hibiscus involving a stunning combination of coronet and braided chignon. Easily twenty-five years my senior, this close friend of Father's never failed to please with beauty and charm and that night proved no different. I caught her blue eyes gazing in my direction and proceeded at once to go to greet her.

As I clutched her waist and kissed her cheek, she whispered of the delight she had felt when previously hearing of my safe return from the war.

"I was not as familiar with your father as I wanted to be, but it is too late now. All I have of him are a few delicious memories and you standing here now."

"A man of many mysteries, my father."

"I miss him. He knew of everything happening in New Orleans and of quite a few interesting things happening well beyond—secret knowledge. And now here we are on this night after so many years. You've changed."

"And you, madame, are more beautiful than ever."

Arm-in-arm we made for the dance floor where we whirled together among the amorous crowd for a multitude of dances during the long night. She wanted to be shared with others only as necessary.

"Is it not boorish of me to keep you so much to myself tonight?"

"I am a widow and no longer a young woman; I shall dance with whom I desire as often as I desire. But why me when you can have most any of the young, vivacious debutantes here tonight?"

"They do not interest me in the least."

"Drouet, I've heard things about you."

"Do you approve of what you have heard?"

"The stories I hear are riveting. I always approve of riveting."

"Then we comprise the offices of chairman and co-chairman of our own mutual admiration society. Pray, what have you heard of yours truly?"

"I hear you still cast your lot with a society responsible for certain national conspiracies, and I hear you are quite proficient with knives."

"And what else?"

"That you perform arm-in-arm with a certain Loreta Velazquez, formerly a top agent in New Orleans of said society. A dangerous lady by all accounts. Also, that you and Loreta are privy to great Confederate secrets."

"You don't wonder that these stories might be slightly exaggerated?"

The widow St. Croix answered only with a coy chuckle.

"Let's cease discussing this dreary war-time business, shall we?"

"Then what shall we talk about, Drouet?"

"Let's concentrate on how delightful it is to be in your company."

The dances continued apace, the Sazeracs flowed almost as heavily as the waters of the mighty Mississippi, and the hours passed to early the next morning with a sky still dark with night.

Loreta and I crossed paths again as St. Croix and myself finished our last dance. Loreta greeted us both.

"Drouet, you two made a handsome couple tonight."

"Loreta, you performed well yourself. I admire you even more after your footwork tonight."

We exchanged stories for several minutes before noticing that we were among the few remaining revelers in the great ballroom. We made it to the foyer and outer doorway when I told Loreta I must return inside to retrieve my cape. Having reclaimed my garment, I then walked back to the foyer near the doorway. Loreta saw me, smiled, and then walked out to the cobblestone walkway outside the theater.

Just as she made her right turn outside the doorway, a man approached her from the darkness.

"Mrs. Williams, or should I say Miss Velazquez, it has been a long time."

I decided to remain hidden inside the foyer for the time being.

"Mr. Winslow, you're a long way from your bureaux at the treasury in Washington City, and, yes, it has been a long time. Happy Mardi Gras."

"You rebels and your vile Mardi Gras. Give us time, and it will be no more. The south's new overlords will bring righteousness to this hellish den one day."

"How did you know to find me here? And why do you call me Velazquez?"

"It took me some time to deduce your true identity of Velazquez, but I did. I also learned you sort of hail from this devilish haunt, so I knew that if you were in New Orleans, you would definitely be at this ball tonight."

"Why do you want to see me?"

"You surely know exactly why I want to see you. Let's discuss your time working for Lafayette Baker, shall we?"

"I served him with distinction. He announced as much to all of Washington City."

"You know as well as I that Baker was as corrupt if not more so than the very scoundrels he rooted out of the treasury, and that's how you came to manipulate him so effectively. He only wanted to bring justice upon criminals reaping the profits that he desired for himself."

"I know nothing of that."

"You know a great deal about quite a lot, I'm sure, Miss Velazquez. I will bring you to the Federal authorities here in New Orleans, and we shall discuss these matters at great length."

"I'm afraid that you mystify me, sir. I'm at a disadvantage, not at all aware of that which you speak."

"Don't play that game with me. You were a rebel spy and an agent of the K.G.C., and I often suspected you as such during those days. When you left abruptly at war's end after Baker mentioned to you that Velazquez had been suspected in the assassination attempt, then the epiphany struck."

"How do you know that he mentioned that to me?"

"He told me as much. Then I asked where the lovely Mrs. Williams had gotten off to so suddenly. Then I began backtracking your history with the agency, looking over all of your activities, and it became apparent that you are likely the true Loreta Velazquez."

"Baker would attest to my loyalty to this day."

"Please, Baker was a bully, a simple thug, a crook who had a name for abusing his power, and his real boss in Washington City, secretary Stanton did not care."

"Sir, Mr. Baker and his brother, Luther, were responsible for capturing Lincoln's killer."

"Were they? Mr. Baker sure knew how and where to find Booth when tasked with the job by Secretary Stanton, didn't he? He knew exactly along which roads to look and exactly in which area of Virginia to search. With knowledge of Booth's personal diary, he instructed Luther to return to Washington City swiftly after cornering Booth the assassin. Funny, isn't it? And then the diary was, in fact, returned, but with eighteen pages missing. What was written on those eighteen pages? How did Lafayette Baker seem to know at once where to find the assassins? Was the content of these missing eighteen pages in any way related to the seemingly supernatural tracking powers possessed by the brothers Baker? For all of their great hunting prowess, both Lafayette and Luther were handsomely rewarded, and the affair was then tidied up in the most convenient fashion . . . just like that."

"You still have not told me what I have to do with any of these wild speculations."

"That's just it. I'm not precisely sure of your exact involvement, just that I highly suspect you know something about it at the very least. You see, I have a lot of questions that I think the government would want answered if only someone would apprise them of the information. Questions such as, 'How did Baker have so much information about Booth's whereabouts immediately after the assassination? And not just the whereabouts of Booth, but also of his co-conspirators immediately upon being tasked with the job by Stanton?' Questions such as, 'Why did someone familiar with Booth state that the body pulled from the barn did not resemble that of John Wilkes Booth?' Questions such as, 'Who was the mysterious lady seen with Booth reconnoitering the alleyway behind Ford's Theater before the assassination?' I believe that lady to be you, Loreta Janeta Velazquez. I also believe you have probably apprised your Confederate friend Broussard of most all of your activities. He's also on my list for bagging. I hate to ruin your night of debauchery, Miss Velazquez, but I'm taking you in right now."

From my secret spot in the dark foyer behind the door, I heard all of this and knew that the time for me to act had arrived. I reached deep into my cape, clutched my blades and stepped outside just in time to see Loreta, derringer in hand, blast Mr. Winslow to somewhere beyond the veil. The crack of gunfire filled the night, followed by an eerie silence.

Loreta and I locked gazes momentarily before I quickly lifted the body of the deceased over my shoulder and extracted him from the scene at once.

Having carried Winslow's body deep into the darkness of a nearby alleyway, Loreta and myself emptied his pockets thoroughly so as to remove any items that could give away his identity.

"Loreta, get yourself and that derringer as far from here as you can as fast as you can. I will meet you back at the apartment when I have hidden this cargo."

"What are you going to do with it?"

"Never you mind right now, but you will learn in due course. Just know that I intend that this body never shows again in the light of day."

After retrieving our carriage from the valet at the main door of the theater, I drove it by hook and by crook to the alleyway where lay the unfortunately curious Mr. Winslow, loaded him onto the coach and proceeded to Lafayette Cemetery. Only a few times en route did reveling onlookers notice the slumped over body and ask questions. Each time I answered that my friend enjoyed the revelry of the evening just a little too much and that I endeavored to return him safely home before the gray light of dawn fell upon us.

Mr. Winslow and I entered the main gate of Lafayette Cemetery and proceeded to the same tomb housing the loot from the mint building heist. Looking first one way and then another to ascertain the possible presence of any unwanted company, and finding none, I worked open the backside of the tomb, crawled inside and rearranged as best I could the bags of treasure placed there by me so long ago. Having made room for our guest, I then crawled out, grabbed him up and hauled him to the opening. It took some doing, but I shoved him inside and made him as comfortable as I could, re-sealed the opening and made for home.

Along the way, I pondered the events of the night and my next course of action. I decided to come back to Lafayette Cemetery the following night, pull out the body from its temporary residence and transport it to a more permanent home.

I rested easy knowing no one would find the missing Mr. Winslow in the interim.

The following day I made arrangements for the work ahead that night involving Mr. Winslow's permanent sequester. That involved securing a boat for passage across the river and a wagon with a false bottom awaiting me on the other side to use for a twenty-mile journey south of New Orleans to a point in the swamps known only to me and two very close friends, two brothers to whom we shall refer only as Armand and Thibaut.

Once the darkness of night had fully set in, I arrived at Lafayette Cemetery aboard the very same false-bottomed wagon Loreta, and I had used for the mint heist. I pulled the wagon to a spot as close to the back of the tomb as possible, opened the rear gate of the wagon and went to work. Having opened the rear passageway into the tomb, I then pulled Mr. Winslow from within and tightly wrapped his body in wide strips cut from bed sheets earlier that day. Once Mr. Winslow had taken on something of a mummified state, I knew the time had come. I hoisted him underneath the false bottom of the wagon, hitched the gate and looked all around in the darkness and determined the moment a most opportune time to make for the river.

I took a roundabout route to the river, using the loneliest thoroughfares, the darkest alleyways, through areas seldom frequented by police or by any number of unwelcome Yankee soldiers still roaming the city blocks.

Mr. Winslow and I made it to our spot on the river with no interruptions along the way. My river contact had been waiting on me and knew exactly what to do when we arrived. He helped me load the body onto his wooden boat, and we stepped aboard, shoved off and began rowing our way across the wide river.

Once on the other side, we pulled the boat aground, off-loaded Mr. Winslow and waited for my next contact to arrive with the second false-bottomed wagon of the night, an event which happened just a few minutes after our arrival, as he had been waiting and watching for us in the nearby brush and trees.

We carried our friend to the wagon parked some thirty yards distant. Mr. Winslow now lay concealed beneath the false bottom. Atop the false bottom, in public view, lay assorted fishing poles, nets and baskets—the everyday belongings of a Cajun fisherman living in the vicinity.

Thus began the longest leg of the night's journey. The driver, who I shall call Everard, knew our next destination intimately, having grown up there some twenty miles from the Crescent City in the swamps alongside the alligators, water moccasins and swamp rabbits. We traveled along together in silence, each aware of the business at hand.

In spite of the unpleasant purpose of the night's activities, the sights, scents, and sounds along the lonely road served as a welcome, but an all-too-brief get away from the recent ugly business and bustle associated with my hometown.

We made our way along the main road for many miles before veering onto a narrower, more desolate trace over which we traveled another five miles or so. Finally, at the end of the trail, we beheld a remote log cabin underneath the moonlight. Armand and Thibaut awaited inside, as evidenced by the dim lantern light within.

Everard approached the cabin and knocked on the front door. Armand and Thibaut answered at once, both their silhouettes showing against the background of the yellow lantern light shining from inside the abode. Once Armand and Thibaut knew the identity of their guests and the greetings had been exchanged, Everard and I were invited inside where the alligator and crawfish were served in abundance, and the bourbon flowed freely.

I told my old friends of life in the Confederate service in Indian Territory, and they allowed how happy they were to see me back home safe and sound. Of my life over the last several years, I informed them of the matters I could and refrained from divulging any particulars that I couldn't. Everard, Armand, and Thibaut seemed to know I held back certain details, appreciating the information offered forth while not prying into certain concerns left only partially explained.

After several hours of catching up, dining on swamp food and swallowing bourbon, the time to finish the job lay upon us. We all walked out to the wagon and off-loaded the late Mr. Winslow and set him underneath an ancient live oak at the back of the cabin. Armand and Thibaut explained that the former national detective staffer should be close to perfect alligator food after percolating for nearly two days. They explained that he might have to season another day or so underneath the sun to arrive at just the right scent favored by a couple of man-eaters living nearby. Further, they both allowed that I could return to New Orleans assured of their expert supervision in the matter.

After bidding our adieus, Everard and I boarded the wagon and made our way back along the same indirect pathways as before, this time back in the direction of the river and New Orleans. We arrived at the river and, once again, I stepped into the wooden boat, and across the river we rowed until we reached the other side. I eventually made it back to Loreta and the dark, dank alleyways of the Vieux Carre.

During the trip back to New Orleans, a strong premonition enveloped me, an awareness that somehow, in some as yet unknown manner, the ever continuing and unfolding story of Lincoln's assassination lay before me in ways that jeopardized not only Loreta's life but also my own.

Soon enough, the lights, laughter, and life of the Vieux Carre pressed those ominous foreshadowings from my brain as I found myself back on familiar streets and alleyways.

Even in the early hours of the morning, with the gray of dawn rapidly approaching, the sound of a tin-panny piano

echoed from a distant saloon, and more than a handful of dedicated revelers showed themselves on the streets.

Now, lest one thinks I viewed the matter concerning Mr.
Winslow a bit too flippantly, let me attest that I fully understood that the former national detective agency staffer only
sought to expose the truth regarding the assassination of
Abraham Lincoln. I will not deny the honor such an endeavor
suggests for a man from the north, but not for one minute
would I have allowed the right honorable gentleman to drag
Loreta Janeta Velazquez before any Yankee officials in New
Orleans to suffer any number of possible undesirable outcomes
resulting from such an inquisition.

And I certainly did not intend that his body turn up again
to raise the specter of that unfortunate incident outside the
Gaiety-Variete Theater in the dark hours of the morning
following a most memorable Mardi Gras ball of 1866.

If she hadn't killed him, I would have.

13

MARIE LAVEAU PREDICTS THE FUTURE

No FURTHER ATTACKS FROM THE DARKNESS BEFELL ME for the time being. My blades had remained tucked in my cape, and it pleased me that the occasions requiring their use had ceased. Perhaps, I thought, no such further surprises lay in my immediate future.

The gris-gris Marie Laveau gave me had worked its magic. During my previous meeting with the elderly yet alluring mystic, she told me, "... you must kill them before they kill you." Then she asked that I visit her again after the task had been completed.

I intended to pay the mystic grand lady of New Orleans a call not only because I promised to, but also because I wanted to out of affection and respect. My visit came to fruition about two weeks after Mardi Gras when I had grown assured that all loose ends related to the Winslow affair had been tied permanently.

Marie's equally beautiful and mysterious daughter met me at the door of their residence on St. Ann Street and led me inside to the elder Laveau who smiled and motioned me to sit at the round table just inside the foyer.

"I knew you would call very soon and probably today. I know you have been busy, and I knew you would be after I saw you last time."

"I have been."

"You see fewer shadow people these days."

"How do you know this?"

"Because as I grow older and my eyes fail me, my inner eye grows stronger all the while. I can barely see you sitting next to me, but I see much more than I ever have in the murky darkness."

"You wanted me to see you after I felt certain I had finished those who waited for me in the shadows."

"Yes, and I know you have completed your work well. I see and hear things while sitting here at night. I see visions. I even hear your curses as you work with your blades in the dark of night by the river."

"The blades might become a habit. I don't like it."

"You should have little use for them in the coming years, but carry them regardless."

"I also don't like seeing the shadow people. I sometimes fear them more than those who once charged at me in battle not long ago."

"And fear them you should. They bring nothing good to any man. But the shadow people are not done with you."

"Why is that?"

"You will meet a man with the mark of death upon him, a man with no good end awaiting him. He seeks your help, and you will give it, but it does not change his final outcome. A man gets what he gives."

"Should I fear this man?"

"No, but do fear the shadows who walk with him. They swarm around him in legions."

"When will I see this man?"

"I do not know the date or the time or the place. But I have seen him in my dreams here as I sit and drink my chicory."

Laveau's daughter then broke in, handing me a cup from the same pot from which her mother drank.

"You missed our Mardi Gras celebration."

"I'm sorry I missed it. I meant to drop by after I left the Gaiety-Variete Theater. Something came up unexpected."

"Something related to what you and Mother discuss?"

"Perhaps."

"You missed a wonderfully delicious and lively soiree. It was scrumptious. I'm sure you know many who were there. I know, you had to be at the Comus affair, but I'm sure it couldn't compare."

"Hearing your guests shriek with pleasure is more fun than doing what I did, I'm sure. Mine was a most tedious business that night."

Just then, I paid notice to an assortment of photographs laying on the table before me. The very high-quality photographs showcased nothing but children of African descent dressed in their finest.

Leaveau the younger smiled as I held several of the images for closer inspection.

"Those are wonderful, aren't they?"

"What are they for?"

"Those in the photographs are recently-freed slave children. We are selling the photographs to folks up north to raise money to school them."

"How much are you fetching for a photograph?"

"Twenty-five cents for the small ones, as much as one-dollar for the big ones. Phillip Bacon is the man organizing this. Have you heard of him?"

I replied that I had.

The name Phillip Bacon began making its rounds in New Orleans some years previous. Originally from Connecticut, Bacon made his way to the Crescent City with the Yankee army that eventually occupied it. He had lately made a name as a cotton and sugar planter on two leased plantations and had done well up to that point. Many knew him as a friend to former slaves and as an advocate for their formal schooling.

"Drouet, Mama knows all about Mr. Bacon. He's raising money for the new school. He knows folks up north who love buying these photographs."

"I see why. They are of the highest quality, little works of art. How can one not love them?"

"Then you should buy some."

"You convinced me. I think I will. How about I purchase everything on the table here?"

I set a gold coin on the table and told her to use it toward the school. Laveau the younger began stacking the photographs in orderly stacks.

"How about you keep those and sell them to another?"

Laveau the younger smiled, and I knew she stood well-pleased. I remember feeling pleasantly curious at both of the Laveau's passion for providing schools for recently-freed slave children and for children of recently freed slaves.

Marie brought me another cup of chicory, this time laced with warm milk, and sat herself at the round table.

We spoke of many things—of my late father, of my forth-coming visitor, of shadow people, of schools for little African children formerly slaves, of our ever-changing New Orleans, of parties of old and those yet to come, and of the spell she had cast upon my enemies known and unknown when she had heard I left for the Indian Territory some years previous. She asked if I carried my gris-gris and I pulled it from my cape pocket to prove I did. She smiled at the sight of it, and I knew she felt well-pleased.

She then took the gris-gris and placed it upon the altar covered with a statue of St. Anthony and images of other saints. She set lit candles around the gris-gris and spoke words so softly and silently that I barely heard them. Its protective powers now enhanced, she returned the gris-gris and said that I now walked with an even greater shield than before, but to keep my eyes opened and my blades sharpened nevertheless.

Then, once again, I remembered Father's words to me concerning the K.G.C. shortly before he died:

"Just slither within its ranks as unnoticed as possible, play the game, play it smart, wait it out until the end, and, when the end comes, as it most certainly will come, have yourself situated on the other side of the world if possible."

I had tried to carry out his instructions as best I could throughout the war and in its aftermath, a time which found the South weakened in defeat and the clandestine cabal that had successfully agitated for the great clash weakening with each passing day.

Laveau gave me to believe that the end of the game might be near, that certain matters might be brought to bear ending my involvement in this contest not of my making. From behind those dark and alluring eyes of Father's mystic friend, a friend now also mine, the events of my future played out as if on a great theatrical stage, and that future included the specter of a mysterious visitor with the mark of death upon him and around whom swarmed a legion of shadow people.

For some reason, seeing the Laveau ladies induced a need for retrospection on my part. I thought back on many of the events of recent years, but most notably of The Circle and the great assignments it demanded of me, of near-impossible tasks such as robbing the mint building, which, had I been caught in that act, would have landed me in prison. Adding insult to injury, the secret order then issued me orders on how the money should be dispersed and when. The secret society had successfully enlisted the entire country to fight their war for them, and fight these men did until the finest of their ranks from both north and south ended dead upon the battlefields—a complete waste. I allowed myself no better or smarter than the unfortunate pawns from both sides who did their bidding.

Having grown tired of acting the pawn, I vowed just then that those days had ended.

Henceforth, I viewed the treasure at Lafayette Cemetery as proceeds for anything and anyone I might personally choose. After all, I devised the plan and took all the risks of the operation to see the plan through successfully. Then, I hid away the loot in the choicest hiding spot in all of New Orleans under the noses of everyone. Why should I not enjoy the spoils of my risks successfully taken, of my labor and of my ingenuity? In what part of the mint heist operation did any of the remaining K.G.C. overlords participate? What risks had they incurred giving them moral authority in the matter?

Leaving the Laveau residence on St. Ann Street, my mind gave thought to those and a handful of other questions. What tomorrow held I knew not, but I had people to visit, glasses of Sazerac to savor, and a crypt to visit at Lafayette Cemetery.

The next night found me at the aforementioned City of the Dead on a withdrawal visit. In the dark of a moonless night, I made my way there afoot, fearing the clip-clop of horse hooves en route might attract unwanted attention. I made my way to the main entrance and pulled up short, stopping to let my eyes, ears, and nose detect what they might from that vantage point.

Assured that no one lurked in the shadows, I floated along

as quietly as possible to the cache site, just as silently removed the stones from the rear of the ossuary and, while positioned face down on the soil, crept within. Once inside I lit a match to see what choice treasures I might extract for a good cause. Having identified several topnotch bags and more than one handsome ingot, I bagged said booty and crawled out. As always, I moved the rear stones back in place in such a way that no one could ever perceive their temporary removal. I then lit another match to illuminate the ground around me to check for any evidence of my visit. Finding none, I crept first along one aisle and then down another, in between vaults in one section and around several tombs in another.

Once at the main gate, I turned for a final look back inside the metropolis of the departed for a sign of anyone still lurking on this side of the veil and spied nothing of the sort. I've often seen shadow people, and more than once I've sensed other-worldly spirits in my presence, but never have I shuddered while in their midst.

Those still living concern me more.

The living oftentimes carry knives and shooting irons and intend to draw blood.

I bade farewell to those beyond the veil at Lafayette Cemetery and began my trek to the Vieux Carre.

The following day found me at the Canal Street office of Phillip Bacon, carpetbagger, educator, recent planter and champion of the freedmen. He attended to matters in his office only once monthly, a fact I ascertained earlier, and so there he sat scribbling at his desk when I strode through the front door.

I intended to make an anonymous donation from the benevolent K.G.G. with the gold benefitting the lives of recently-freed slaves and their children.

Without lifting pen from pad, Bacon looked up at me from behind his spectacles just as the front door closed behind me.

He looked more the educator than planter in his tweed trousers, wire-rimmed eyeglasses and brown hair parted evenly down the middle of his head.

His immediate jitteriness indicated my presence disturbed him. He sat frozen with wide eyes as if he beheld the devil himself. His pen still pressed against the exact spot on the pad as when I entered, he managed a greeting.

"Uh, uh, greetings I'm sure, sir."

"Do I stand before Phillip Bacon?"

"You, you do, sir. How may I help you?"

"We have mutual friends, you and I."

"We do? Who might they be, may I ask?"

"The mother and daughter Laveau, Mr. Bacon."

"Ah, yes, an interesting pair those two, as well as their followers, adherents to a dark religion and dark ways, and much in need of education and enlightenment. How do you know them?"

"How do I know them? I've known them from my earliest days as a boy here in New Orleans. I count them as friends. Their religion and their ways are their business and none of my own."

"Surely you don't condone their religious practices, their rituals, their raucous gatherings, their animalistic celebrations."

"I make it my habit to leave people to their chosen indulgences and me to my own. As for their social merrymakings, I've attended a few of their observances with myself as guest."

"Have you not witnessed their indulgences as you call it at Congo Square? Those spectacles resemble something straight from the pit. Only in New Orleans are such exhibitions as those tolerated. You say you have attended these horrible affairs?"

"More than once, as I said."

Bacon, still jittery, eyes still opened as large as the silver dollars extracted from the mint building, sat motionless and silent as he beheld the length and breadth of me standing on the other side of his oak desk. I almost asked if he beheld an apparition next to me.

"New Orleans seems quite needful of the piety native to my land. I see we have much work to do down here."

While finding the carpetbagger's tone disagreeable and annoying, I chose to let it go without remark.

"Well, Mr. Bacon, in your quest to find potential converts in the Crescent City I bid you nothing but happy hunting. Perhaps what I lay before you will help in your righteous and upright endeavors."

With that, I set my briefcase on his desk, opened the latch and began extracting booty retrieved from Lafayette Cemetery the night before. In a matter of less than a minute, assorted bags filled with coins along with various ingots lay strewn on Bacon's desk.

"What say you, sir? Here is my contribution to the virtuous efforts you have planned for the lowly city I call home if you accept?"

I hadn't thought it possible for Bacon's body to seize any tighter or his eyes to grow even larger than before, but I witnessed such as he beheld the loot placed before him. His presence reeked of both shock and incredulity at once, topped off with a strong suggestion of suspicion. It took some few minutes for him to manage an utterance.

"Where, may I ask, did you obtain all of this?"

"If used in the virtuous pursuits with which your name has become synonymous, does the origin of this contribution matter that greatly to you?"

"I ask you directly: Where did you come by it?"

"What if I told you that I stole it from the United States mint in Washington City? What if I told you it came from a federal supply wagon robbed by Confederates up in Indian Territory, and maybe I robbed it from them?"

"I don't know you, sir, and I don't know quite what to make of you. I am inclined to turn over all of this to the authorities."

"Take what I have given you and employ it as you see fit. As for turning this over to the authorities, I highly recommend you refrain from that action. We are in a time of reformation and new beginnings. Use the gold wisely, compassionately and without condemnation."

Tipping my hat, I made for the door.

14

DIVVYING THE SPOILS

You'll pardon me if I omit exact dates when recounting what follows. I do so mainly to protect the innocent and also, in some cases the guilty.

Just know that in the months and years ahead I played host in New Orleans to a veritable who's who of characters who had employed their skills on behalf of the Knights of the Golden Circle throughout the country before, during and after the great war. During these meetings, I handed them packages containing checks, cash, names and addresses of other K.G.C. contacts, their aliases, code words and signals to use in gaining entrance to various "castles" controlled by the cabal, and other information necessary for these individuals to navigate freely and without suspicion for the rest of their lives. When necessary—and only when necessary—I plucked stash from Lafayette Cemetery in the dark of night with which to help pay off these agents.

I emphasize the words "when necessary" because having something of that treasure left over for yours truly at the end of my K.G.C. career never ceased to be my ultimate goal. I allowed, somewhat reluctantly, that an occasional withdrawal from the stash aided me in getting to the peaceful end of said career all the quicker.

About many of my visitors you have no doubt read, and of their exploits you have either cheered or jeered depending on your predisposition on such matters one way or the other.

Frank James' visit proved noteworthy not only because it rekindled our association from years earlier when I helped with the Ohio train robbery, but also because it afforded me first-hand accounts of the James Gang's many colorful exploits in the service of the society since that job.

Many of his stories spoke of K.G.C. plunder still buried in precise locations across Missouri, Kansas, Arkansas and, mostly, Indian Territory, a region familiar to yours truly due to my service there on behalf of General Watie and his fighting Confederate Indians.

We originally met at the Pickwick, but Mr. James felt uncomfortable in its refined environs, so we departed to the bar at Maggie Thompson's brothel on Customhouse Street in the red-light district. After I had made the proper introductions, Mr. James settled in and seemed to feel right at home.

"This is more like it, Broussard. I get a little fidgety around uppity folks, even if they are uppity folks friendly to the former Confederate States. This is more to my liking, right here."

"Think nothing of it. Maggie always says, 'Any friend of Drouet Broussard is a friend of mine.'"

"Didn't know what to think of you when we rode together on that Ohio job, Broussard. To be honest, me and Jesse thought you were a little standoffish back then, but it turned out you knew how to get the job done. Doesn't surprise me none at all that you can fit in at a place like that Pickwick Club."

"I've fit in there for quite a while, but I pride myself on blending in anywhere with anybody."

"I don't doubt that none at all. Me and Jesse later heard about some of your work down in the Indian Territory whilst you fought with them Indians. Impressive work. Leastways, it shore is good to see you again. We've rode the trails and crossed the rivers together."

As most everyone knows, the James Gang's penchant for raiding federal wagon trains and railroad cars acquired during the war continued unabated for many years afterward. According to Frank James, they "appropriated" only as much of the loot for themselves as absolutely necessary and buried the rest in precise, recorded spots for retrieval later by K.G.C. operatives. Part of my job during these meetings involved learning of these various cache sites and reporting said locations up the ladder to my unnamed and unknown superiors.

As mentioned earlier, the rocks and dirt of Indian Territory held a sizeable amount of James Gang stash, and many were Frank's stories involving their jobs in that region. Jesse knew how to separate the little garrisons there from their money when opportunity arose.

Take the case of Fort Arbuckle located in the southernmost region of Indian Territory. One day a heavily guarded caravan of federal wagons left Fort Leavenworth in Kansas carrying payroll for the troops stationed at the little bastion near Mill Creek not too many miles north of the Red River. The caravan had traveled all the way across the territory and found itself within only a few miles of Fort Arbuckle when a flurry of rifle fire took the federal guards by surprise.

In the ensuing fight, five of the men assisting the James Gang were killed, but all of the federals guarding the payroll were wiped out. The gang descended upon the wagons forthwith, lifted the gold from within before setting fire to the entire caravan to suggest an Indian attack. The gang members, anticipating immediate pursuit from Fort Arbuckle troops once they discovered the scene of the attack, knew they had to travel fast, which meant they had to lighten their load. Thus, they decided to hide the gold along three different spots along Mill Creek as they departed the vicinity.

Frank James explained that each hole held almost exactly one-third of the total take. He then explained to me the locations of the three cache sites citing prominent landmarks nearby and accepted K.G.C. symbols carved on trees and chiseled on boulders adjacent the burial spots.

I transcribed all of this information into a journal to send up the K.G.C. ladder later but also storing it away in my mind for possible retrieval myself.

Then James laid before me detailed accounts of robberies about which we in New Orleans had read in newspaper accounts since the end of the war, raids for which authorities still sought culprits.

James laid out in detail how the gang looted the Alexander Mitchell and Company Bank in Lexington, Missouri, how much the raid garnered, the amount they took for themselves and the amount they stashed away for the society and the location of the cache. James went on to explain in detail a long list of robberies, raids, and holdups, how much each adventure harvested, roughly how much the gang members kept to use for operating expenses, and how much they buried in the ground across the countryside and the exact location of each cache. I listened with genuine interest while jotting down extensive notes.

James also explained a habit the gang had for venturing into Mexico looking for looting opportunities. More than once, James said, the gang met in El Paso or any number of other towns near the Rio Grande, to plan heists below the border.

Not all of the raids proved successful, but enough of them did for the gang to manage a hefty overall take over the last several years.

Mexican guards hauling government gold bullion proved the gang's favorite target while operating down there. James mentioned numerous such raids below the border, but I could only recall reading about one of these excursions in the newspapers, a fact which gave me to know that the James Gang successfully covered their tracks while in Mexico. Their biggest challenge often proved escaping back across the border into the United States with their lives.

Once back on the northern side of the border, the gang set aside their take and then went to work burying the remaining treasure in cache sites across Texas and Indian Territory. The gang favored operating in Indian Territory because its environs were often beyond the reach of any lawful authorities. At that time, the few men carrying badges in Indian Territory were often doing the work of the Cherokees, Choctaws, Chickasaws, Creeks, and Seminoles, and the gang members enjoyed friendly associations with many of those officers and did not feel threatened while in their midst.

That is why the James Gang knew most every nook and cranny in Indian Territory. They especially preferred cache sites in the Wichita and Ouachita Mountains of that region. I paid careful attention as James recounted the cache spots because I also stood familiar with the Indian Territory and could navigate there as well as anyone. One never knows what tomorrow holds, and I could wind up needful of said resources just as much as anyone else.

James mentioned Tarbone Mountain in the Wichita Mountains. He mentioned the Fort Sill area not far from there. He described cache sites in those locales and in places with names like Sugarloaf Mountain, Horsethief Springs, Younger's Bend and Robber's Cave.

With detailed description, James continued to relate cache locations along the Arkansas and Poteau Rivers in that region, in the bottomland and cane breaks between Skullyville and Fort Smith, and at any number of different spots in the Ozark foothills near Tahlequah.

DURING HIS FIRST visit to New Orleans, James allowed that he enjoyed the Crescent City, its people, its warm climate and intimated that he could end his days as a criminal and make an honest living in New Orleans. Eventually, through a connection of mine, I helped him find employment at the New Orleans Fair Grounds race track as a betting commissioner.

Mr. James told some remarkable stories to me that day, and I visited with him later, and he recounted even more, but I cannot say that the James Gang's exploits on behalf of the K.G.C. proved the most incredible to me during those days.

Another visitor eventually arrived in New Orleans and narrated an account belonging to the ages.

15

SHADOW PEOPLE ALL AROUND

ONE DAY WHILE WALKING THROUGH THE VIEUX CARRE, I spied a friend from the Pickwick Club waving to me from the front of that establishment. I walked across the street and followed him inside where we took seats in a private meeting room.

My friend and Circle contact, who shall continue to remain unnamed, placed his right forefinger over his mouth to indicate we both speak in the softest of tones.

What he communicated to me on that day ran thus:

A certain John St. Helen had arrived in New Orleans recently where he took up temporary residence with an unnamed family near Camp and First Streets. Without revealing the identity of the family, I freely admit that the late patriarch of said family had been a close friend and business associate of my father. An appointment had been arranged for me to meet with St. Helen only a few nights hence. The appointed late-night hour had been set with instructions for me to arrive and leave in as concealed a manner as possible. Before setting out to the residence on the appointed night, my instructions said to stop by the Pickwick and retrieve a packet intended for our guest. I should approach a certain side door to the residence and, upon arriving, knock at the door using a certain number and cadence of taps. St. Helen's instructions were to remain at said residence for the duration of his visit, never to venture out into the streets or otherwise enjoy the charm of the Crescent City in any way. Other unnamed contacts were charged with eventually whisking St. Helen out of the home and onto a boat on the river at some appointed time after our meeting. Neither St. Helen nor myself could mention the visit ever again unless we desired an assassin's bullet or blade at an unexpected hour, date and place after the fact.

I understood with crystal clarity the subterfuge of the circumstance.

I also remembered that I had met a John St. Helen up in the Indian Territory at General Watie's camp and that I had once overheard Loreta mention the same name while dancing at the Comus Mardi Gras ball. I fully expected to see the man from Indian Territory when I visited the residence at Camp and First Streets in the dark of night a few nights ahead.

At once I recalled the John St. Helen from Watie's camp. I recollected a commanding presence built on charming demeanor, on eloquence with words, and on an expressive physical manner in which he carried himself. When my mind wandered back to the time I met St. Helen at Watie's tent, I felt there seemed to be something more to the man, something I couldn't identify.

I asked myself several questions.

What meaning could I ascribe to having first seen St. Helen in the Indian Territory and how could that same man be in New Orleans right now for the sole purpose of meeting with me?

What did Loreta know about John St. Helen?

What actions had St. Helen carried out that he now required one of the usual envelopes filled with checks, cash, and instructions for the future?

It is a small world, I thought, *but not so small that I should likely encounter the same mysterious man in two different worlds.* Such could be explained as mere coincidence, but I had grown to understand there are seldom such genuine coincidences in this life. A common thread to all of this lurked in the shadows waiting to show itself, and I longed to see the phantom manifest.

The appointed night arrived, and I made my way afoot to the vicinity of Camp and First. 'Twas an overcast night without a moon and the walk I made in the shadows proved quiet and uneventful. Still, as I came within sight of the appointed residence, I increasingly felt watched and followed. I grew leery that something lurked around every corner.

Then, the source of my worry revealed itself.

Shadow people.

Scores of shadow people.

I saw their vague outlines along the street near the home, along the immediate edges of the structure itself, on the roof, clinging to the outer walls. Then, suddenly, the words of Marie Laveau proved true, actually came to life, for she had mentioned that shadow people should accompany one of my upcoming visitors and her menacing words seemed to portend that I should beware the man upon whom they clung.

Through the darkness, I strode to the appointed side door which lay concealed by shrubs and live oaks. I executed the appointed knock on the door, the door opened some few seconds afterward, and a man then unknown to me allowed me entrance. He led me to the base of a winding staircase, and we both commenced stepping upward. Once at the room of the esteemed guest, my host knocked gently on the door, and his taps were answered with, "Please come in."

My host opened the door only slightly ajar and then motioned me inside. After I had entered the room, the door closed behind me, and that is when I focused my attention on the man sitting at a desk to my left.

I then beheld the same man I had met at Watie's camp when last in Indian Territory.

"John St. Helen, I presume, unless my eyes simply fool me into believing you are the same man I saw in Indian Territory long ago."

"Your eyes play no tricks, Broussard. I am that same man. The wheel has come full circle."

He gestured that I be seated.

"I shan't ask about the nature of your business back then, but our very meeting here tonight quite obviously acknowledges our mutual association with the K.G.C. which more than implies our affinity for the cause of southern independence."

"The cause of the K.G.C. lies buried beneath the now cold ashes of history. I know you are smart enough to know that. The cause for southern independence, however, lives on. For now, though, in the south, the sins of the father are to be laid upon the children."

"Who might you be, Mr. St. Helen?"

"Just a man whose allegiances and loyalties gained him naught."

"Your living countenance belies that you are a man who has come to naught."

"I am a simple merchant, a trader."

"My late father was a simple trader—a merchant businessman here in New Orleans, yes, but a trader at his core. You, Mr. St. Helen, are no trader."

"It has been said that the world is but a stage on which

every man plays a part. This is true, and my part has been a sad one. But, Mr. Broussard, I am, in fact, a trader."

"Where do you trade?"

"In Granbury, Texas. I have a store there from which I sell those items most regularly in need by the people there—along with ample supplies of alcoholic spirits and tobacco not so much in need but very much in demand."

"Please describe your establishment."

"There is not much to describe. My store was built of notched logs, very much in the frontier style."

This perplexing man before me belonged most anywhere in the world performing any number of pursuits, but I could not fathom him in the location of Granbury, Texas pursuing retail trade out of a log cabin store.

While acknowledging to myself that he likely did not falsify anything uttered to me up to that point, I strongly suspected he held back hefty amounts of contextual information.

"Mr. St. Helen, I know that everything you have told me is true. Let us get on to matters at hand. I welcome you to the Crescent City."

The comfortable, easy smile St. Helen then formed intimated that he well understood the conflicts and contradictions I sensed when trying to place him in the world he described, and I suddenly realized that he had most certainly encountered this scenario many times before.

"You yourself are a man of many façades, Broussard, and I enjoy our conversation very much. You can ask me anything you like, and I pledge truthfulness in return. I may hold back on directness. Please understand that to be direct and honest is not safe for me or possibly my acquaintances."

His understanding countenance and easy manner fused somehow to create a commanding presence that, complemented by an innate ability to recite words from the Great Bard at will, further took me aback. Perhaps his spoken lines mean little when read by the casual reader, but from the lips of St. Helen the words beautifully rendered the deepest emotion and meaning and garnered for him the undivided attention of anyone in his presence.

"Mr. Broussard, it has taken me much of a wasted lifetime to arrive here, but I have learned to at least try and love all, trust few, and do wrong to none."

"Then we find ourselves on the same page, Mr. St. Helen."

"Call me John."

16

AN INTERVIEW WITH JOHN

As I looked about the room, I quickly ascertained that Mr. St. Helen's movements appeared limited to its confines. Everything he might need to get through the day lay before him, a fact giving him no reason to leave the chamber.

"John, I have to ask, are you confined to this room? I sense you are."

"You discern much, perhaps too much I'm afraid, but yes, my instructions are to remain cloistered between these four walls until departure time a few nights from tonight."

"I understand you will not make the trip back to Texas over land."

"That is true. I shall board a boat for Galveston. There I shall remain at a K.G.C. enclave on Avenue M for a time and from there up to Granbury."

"Would you like to leave here for better environs, for fine dining and glasses of your favorite beverages?"

"I'm afraid we both must follow directives. If I am to receive instructions for the future and the needed resources you have in that envelope, then we must follow orders faithfully."

"You forget two matters of great importance."

"And those are?"

"Firstly, I, Drouet Broussard, possess the envelope you mentioned and you have to be in my company when I actually disperse to you its contents. Secondly, we are both grown men, and I shall handle anyone who might stand between us and the Pickwick Club on this night."

"Many years have elapsed since my last visit there."

"Ah, so you have been there before and must well understand why you cannot leave the Crescent City without visiting that most esteemed haunt off limits to all but a select few. Let us depart at once. You shall be my guest, and we will be most faithfully discreet on our outing. Whose guest might you have been before?"

At that, St. Helen smiled as if he owned a great secret.

"Perhaps I shall tell you in due time."

"Then enough talk. Let us depart these premises at once."

Once outside, we garnered a carriage and began making our way to the Vieux Carre. That night, our steed pulled us along streets most lonesome, through alleyways darkest with shadows, filling the blackness with gentle clip-clops along brick and cobblestone until we arrived at our destination.

Once inside, we found ourselves surrounded by only a handful of members. Several of the members looked at St. Helen with great interest, some as if enchanted by his appearance and movements, others as if they had seen him before, and one or two as if they had seen a ghost. St. Helen seemed aware of the attention, but simply brushed it off with a wry smile and followed me to a corner table out of sight of the onlookers.

St. Helen ordered a whiskey and water and me my beloved

Sazerac. When the drinks arrived at our table, St. Helen raised his glass.

"To quote a good friend of mine, 'I drink to the general joy of the whole table.' So, Broussard, how did you find your way into our illustrious dark society?"

"By way of my late father, one of the founding members, who probably joined more out of allegiance to personal friends, and specifically, to New Orleans society, in general, than for any other reason."

"Interesting. You said your father worked as a merchant and trader, yes? Then, I take it he never had reason to own slaves?"

"Correct."

"And so you joined because your father asked you to?"

"I joined because one of Father's close friends asked me to."

"Who was that?"

"General Albert Pike."

"Well, I will be damned. The picture comes into full view for me now. Your father seems to have enjoyed a select group of personal friends."

"True. I can rattle off more impressive names than that. But Pike deserves credit, or blame depending on one's view, for plucking me from New Orleans and into action first in Indian Territory on behalf of General Watie—in whose presence I saw you when last there—and then eventually into the service of the cabal that joins us here tonight."

"Somehow I get the feeling that you haven't been entirely happy in its service."

"Honestly, as I think back on it more and more, the young Broussard who joined the society some ago did so believing it stood mainly for southern independence more than anything else, and you and I both know that is not true. Might I ask what was your business with Watie when I saw you in his camp at the close of the war?"

"You found me in Watie's camp undercover, and I am afraid that is all I can say about it."

The longer I conversed with St. Helen, the more I believed him somebody more than he presented, but we had barely imbibed a single glass of spirits between the both of us, and I, at that point, allowed that his business remained his own.

St. Helen intimated that he had once harbored now regretful feelings toward the black race and therein lay his reason for joining The Circle many years before.

"I once looked upon Africans as a race belonging in perpetual subjugation to white overlords, but I now know I stood wrongheaded in those days. But you can certainly see why I joined a society completely dedicated to the cause of slavery's expansion to our country's western territories and states, to Mexico and throughout the Caribbean."

I sat quietly and listened thoughtfully to his words, as I, too, had gone through changes in belief as to the validity of the causes championed by the K.G.C.

We passed away the hours speaking of the war, of Reconstruction in New Orleans and throughout the rest of the South, and of the future. The spirits flowed freely, and I gathered that St. Helen valued the conversation and atmosphere as highly as I did and that a certain amount of camaraderie and trust had been established between us.

"The war is long over and the dark society as you call it loses power and influence with each passing day, and so I ask you John St. Helen, who are you?"

"Remember when I said I love all, trust few, and do wrong to none? Well, the 'trust few' part I take most serious of all, and I wager you feel the same when asked to divulge the details of your activities down through the years, especially of those activities on behalf of The Circle. So, let me ask you, Drouet Broussard, who are you and what brings you to this place and time with me here tonight? Let me hear what you have to say and then maybe you might become one of the aforementioned few. Your secrets are safe with me."

I contemplated his request and gave it serious consideration for a few minutes before deciding to lay it before him in no uncertain terms.

My reasons for doing so were four-fold.

First, the K.G.C. found itself closer to irrelevance with each passing day, and I feared the society's ever-shrinking tentacles in equally diminishing measure. Angering anyone in the cabal dense enough to continue clinging to its original cause in the aftermath of the war concerned me not.

Secondly, if St. Helen ever decided to recount my story to authorities, he could offer no certain proof to back up the allegation, and he would certainly place himself at risk for incriminating himself.

Thirdly, if my account helped to glean from St. Helen his back story then all the better.

And, lastly, my instincts told me I could trust St. Helen completely.

"St. Helen, your answer acknowledges you hide something, but you have been as honest with me as you feel you can be, and I don't believe you have lied to me even once. I now lay before you the unvarnished truth as to my activities on behalf of the K.G.C. You may decide for yourself as to the truthfulness of the narrative.

"I told you how I came to join the society, how it transpired out of certain friendships and society connections of my father. I explained how Pike first recruited me to work with the Confederate Indians of Indian Territory, and I did so as a scout and spy. Pike had heard of my accomplishments at the

Louisiana State Seminary of Learning and Military Academy under the direction of Major William Tecumseh Sherman and knew my talents would benefit the cause.

"Prior to that, Pike had personally enlisted the various tribes in eastern Indian Territory into service on behalf of the Confederacy, and therefore I felt an obligation to assist them in any way possible. Pike felt I could help in the field and also keep him abreast of activities on a regular schedule.

"During the war, the intelligence I had gathered proved pivotal in tracking Yankee wagon train and riverboat movements in that region, and when the time came to attack and seize said vehicles, I pulled my weight with the rest of General Watie's riflemen in bringing these strikes to a successful conclusion.

"Watie's example of bold, quick strikes rubbed off on me after several such raids, and I later assisted the James Gang with a raid upon the safes of the Adams Express Company aboard the Ohio and Mississippi railway near Cincinnati, Ohio —an action ordered by the K.G.C. and not by the Confederacy."

With that, St. Helen, now smiling, almost gleeful, broke in.

"I heard about that raid! News of it spread around the entire country, especially in the North! You mean to tell me you were part of that assault, you and the famous Jesse and Frank James?"

"This accounting contains the unvarnished truth, as I promised."

"The country still wonders who carried out that robbery and here I sit with one of the members of that merry band."

St. Helen's wry smile indicated his belief. He leaned forward in his chair with his chin resting in the palm of his left hand.

"I have to hear more. Pray, continue."

"If you enjoy the story of that heist, then you will love the recounting of the one that happened before that. After the battle of Pea Ridge in Arkansas, Pike sent word that I meet him at a secluded cabin near Caddo Gap in the Ouachita Mountains of the southwestern section of that state.

"Upon arrival and while in Pike's company, I took the oath and joined the Knights of the Golden Circle. I then agreed to rob a building here in New Orleans that had served as home to the United States Mint before the war and for a short time as home to the Confederate Mint after the war commenced and the Confederate government had taken control of the premises."

St. Helen, a look of amazement upon his face, stopped me short.

"When did you do this and how did you it?"

"Like Watie, I chose the bold path. I learned that in heists, just as in espionage, one should be so bold as to make one's movements seem natural."

St. Helen, still sporting the same wry smile of belief, chin still resting upon his palm, broke in again.

"I hear certain actors on the stage employ the same device. Please, continue."

"So, on or about late April, 1862, with Yankee warships moving upriver in the direction of New Orleans, with throngs of fear-ridden citizens scurrying about like many thousands of ants fresh out of a toppled anthill, I, along with an able accomplice, robbed the mint building on Esplanade Avenue in the pouring rain. I add that nature seemed to be in agreement with our activities that night, as the weather provided a much-needed layer of concealment and distraction.

"With my accomplice waiting in the wagon, I made multiple trips in and out of the building carrying bags, bullion, and bricks taken from behind a false wall in a closet where it had been planted sometime before by a K.G.C. operative working in the building when it served as the United States Mint.

"The K.G.C. had long known of the stash put there by its operative and the society charged me with getting it out, and I did. These details are fairly the beginning and end of it."

St. Helen leaned back in his chair seemingly satisfied with what he had just heard.

"Just two questions, Broussard. First, who was your accomplice? Second, where is the booty now?"

"You'll understand that I cannot divulge the name of my willing and capable associate that day. As to the location of the takings, I can only say that it is located in proximity of the Crescent City and that you will be partly paid from that handsome pile before you leave for Galveston."

"Drouet Broussard, you have told me everything I needed to hear. I now know you are a man of honor and a man of his word. I needn't know of the location of the takings from the mint building to know you did exactly what you described and how you described it. But, most importantly, you did not give up the name of your collaborator, the beautiful and vivacious Loreta Janeta Velazquez."

At that, my heart began beating harder than it had when knife fighting with the assorted alleyway thugs shortly after the mint heist. Though I trusted St. Helen, I felt an innate urge to protect Loreta.

"I know assorted ladies who have worked on behalf of our little society but, pray, please enlighten me as to this Velazquez for this is the first I have heard of her."

St. Helen, now beaming a smile of immense satisfaction, looked around the room to make sure no one sat within earshot. Then, in a whispered voice, he answered.

"My friend, that seals it. But it's no good, for I know you

have worked intimately close with the lady of whom I speak. Let's just say I have also worked with her. I like her, I admire her, and she is one of the few people in this world whose friendship I cherish. I liked you from the beginning, Broussard, and now I know why. You keep your word, and you protect your friends. Cassius told Brutus that a friend should bear his friend's infirmities, so now I shall tell you who I am and what I have done.

"I am John Wilkes Booth, and I am the assassin of Abraham Lincoln, president of the United States."

17

THE PROFESSED ASSASSIN'S STORY

My years with the society had taught me to sometimes doubt nothing, however far-fetched, while questioning everything, regardless of its apparent plausibility. Sometimes things are not always as they seem, and often-times great revelations are gleaned from reading between the lines of accepted narratives that omit vital information either accidentally or deliberately.

Many might laugh to hear the recounted details of certain exploits of which I had been directly involved or to which I had been privy, as said exploits might seem too fantastic to be believed. My service to the society had been as a relative underling in the grand scheme of things, so what impressive feats had been accomplished by those mysterious notables at the top of the cabal? What strings had they pulled in the highest of places to further the aims of our clandestine fraternity? My own fruitful imagination would surely fall short in contriving all that had passed.

I had met my contact at the Pickwick Club many times to receive information and material necessary to conduct the affairs of this league of schemers. Never once did I know who first gave the sealed packages to him, nor did I know who had supplied his supplier. Truthfully, I had long held as an absolute certainty that many degrees of deniability stood between myself in New Orleans and whoever gave initial orders at the top of our secret apparatus.

In a court of law, how could I implicate anyone above me if I did not know their identity? And how could an operative above me at any level point a finger at his superior if he stood oblivious of his name and whereabouts? Knowing this, let us ask, *How easy might it be, then, for one in the upper echelons to issue an order, however diabolical, and never lose a wink of sleep worrying about his own discovery in the evil enterprise?*

Quite easily, I surmised.

In spite of this knowledge, however, I had to fight back my initial temptation to harshly question my friend's shocking claim. Instead, I posed my first response to it in a more moderate fashion.

"As you know, the government claims that you were shot in a Virginia barn and that your body rests six-feet beneath the clay. Naturally, you'll understand that while I instinctively tend to disbelieve your claim, I do find it quite remarkable and desire greatly to hear the story backing it up."

"I understand your doubt, especially in light of the government in Washington's official story claiming otherwise, as printed in thousands of newspapers across the continent over these many years. But I am happy to describe to you in detail how I came to sit before you now in the Pickwick Club of New Orleans for the purpose of collecting money and information from the organization for which we both have labored successfully. Please digest the information I lay before you and believe me or believe me not. I swear it to be truthful.

"This man before you is John Wilkes Booth, son of the late

Junius Brutus Booth, Sr., the actor, and a brother of Junius Brutus Booth the second and Edwin Booth, the actor.

"As you may already know, I come from a family whose sympathies solidly favored Lincoln's government during the late war. Despite my family's stance for the federal cause, I found myself in possession of strong sympathies for the cause of the southern people, so much that I had completely given up my profession and the study of the art of acting shortly after the war commenced.

"Long before that night at the Ford Theater, I worked on behalf of the Confederate Secret Service with the intention of kidnapping Abraham Lincoln in order to hold him against the release of the many thousands of Confederate soldiers then residing in northern prisons. Once in my hands, I planned to deliver the Yankee president to the Confederate government at Richmond, Virginia to be held as a hostage of war.

"Then, suddenly, on the ninth day of April 1865, Generals Lee and Grant signed the surrender of Confederate forces at Appomattox Courthouse and our plans to kidnap President Lincoln dissolved as so much snow thrown into a fire. Prisoners of war held in both the north and the south would soon be freed and making their way back home.

"Thus, the end of the war necessitated ending the plan to kidnap President Lincoln. War's end also necessitated consideration of the future of the southern people at the hands of the now victorious northern government and the radical abolitionists who controlled it.

"I am an actor by nature, an artist if you will, and not an assassin, and I do not believe I am in possession of a mean heart, but I and others with whom I worked and conspired stood convinced that the death of President Abraham Lincoln and the succession of Vice-President Andrew Johnson of Tennessee to the Yankee presidency stood as the only hope of protecting the southern people from tyrannical rule and the confiscation of their landed estates. Certainly, Johnson had been loyal to the cause of the Yankee government up until then, but he was a southerner by birth and upbringing, and we stood convinced he would not allow for the oppressive rule of the southern people as intended by the abolitionists who controlled President Lincoln.

"However, I had never contemplated taking the life of President Lincoln until the very morning of the day I did so. After several failed attempts to kidnap Lincoln, David E. Herold and myself mounted horses and left Washington City by way of Surrattville using the underground route used so successfully by Confederate spies and scouts throughout the war. Our mission was to perfect one last plan to kidnap the president.

"We made the necessary arrangements for crossing the Potomac and Rappahannock rivers on that route and then returned to Washington City and entered the metropolis on April 14, 1865. At the bridge crossing on the east end of the Potomac River, we were stopped by Yankee troops on guard at that point. We both wondered why these troops stood guard there.

"As it turns out, stories had been circulating throughout Washington City and the countryside all around of planned attempts on the president's life. None of these reports had reached the ears of anyone in our circle of conspirators until then. Based on these accounts, troops had been ordered to monitor the crossing point on the east end of the river and at other points so that no person could enter or exit Washington City without first giving their name and a full account of their business.

"We hesitated in giving our names and were arrested at once. From about eleven o'clock in the morning until two o'clock in the afternoon, we were held in the blockhouse and that is when we first heard about General Lee's surrender at Appomattox Courthouse, news that crushed our spirits and gave us to know that a death blow had been delivered to the Confederacy and to the southern people.

"Our guards let out whoops of glee and their collective mood improved to such a degree that they released us and we were allowed to enter Washington City, but only after we had made a satisfactory account of ourselves."

Thus far in his account, St. Helen, or Booth, had delivered enough detail to fully garner my attention, and I somehow knew that the best of the narrative lay ahead.

"So, you and Herold enter Washington City and go where, exactly?"

"We made a direct beeline to the Kirkwood Hotel."

I then remembered Loreta telling me that she had stayed at the Kirkwood House while in Washington City during her heyday as a double agent on behalf of the Confederate government. She had even confirmed that she met with Andrew Johnson there on several occasions as part of her work.

"Is this Kirkwood Hotel the same establishment as the Kirkwood House? I believe I have heard it mentioned both ways."

"Yes, one and the same, and the longtime rendezvous point of the conspirators against Lincoln."

"Did you ever see Vice-President Andrew Johnson while there?"

"Of course, I saw him. He lived there while in Washington City. In fact, the only reason we conspirators frequented the hotel at all was to meet with Andrew Johnson to lay plans to kidnap President Lincoln, and that is who we went to meet after convincing the troops to allow us entry into the city."

"Then it is likely you brushed by Loreta Velazquez there from time to time."

"Yes, this is also true. I know she is your friend and, as I have said, she is also mine. In fact, back when the plan was to kidnap Lincoln, she went with me to Ford's Theatre and helped me survey the premises as well as the streets and alleyways surrounding it. We established plans for me to make a brisk exit from the area after I had completed my mission there. But, as you know, the plan to kidnap Lincoln never materialized.

"Anyway, when I arrived at the hotel, I called on Vice-President Johnson. We talked about the surrender and how it rendered useless our plans to kidnap President Lincoln and deliver him to the Confederate government in Richmond. We also discussed the sad fate of the southern people who now stood at the heels of the abolitionists who now fully controlled Lincoln and the government in Washington City.

"Johnson's face tightened, and his voice rang with anger and some excitement when he said to me, 'Will you waver at this most supreme moment in history?'

"At first, I did not grasp his meaning and remained silent so he could further explain himself. He did so with a cowardly pale face and quivering lips.

"'You know my meaning, Booth. Do you possess nerve enough to kill him?'

"And now you know from whom came the initial suggestion that President Lincoln be assassinated—from his own vice-president who lusted after the high office himself.

"Johnson then told me he knew of my meeting with Albert Pike, Judah Benjamin and John Slidell in this very club some years before when we originally discussed assassinating Lincoln. While that original plan had evolved into one of kidnapping the president and using him as collateral for gaining freedom for imprisoned Confederate troops, the situation had now changed, and the original plan for assassination could now proceed apace.

"I asked Johnson how he knew of my meeting at the Pickwick with the aforementioned esteemed gentlemen, and he answered that he knew much more than that in his esteemed position in the upper echelons of our secret society.

"I then explained to Johnson that I had been jailed in the blockhouse that very day by Yankee troops on the east end of the river using the Confederate underground route. I feared I could not make good an escape after committing the act as he proposed, as it would then render Washington City a jailed municipality from which no one could escape.

"To this, Johnson said he had read in the newspapers that General and Mrs. U.S. Grant were in the city to be honored that very evening at a guest box in the Ford Theater as guests of the president and Mrs. Lincoln. The president, Johnson said, desired to publicly showcase and congratulate his able general while presenting an image of cooperation and solidarity at this hour of victory.

"I then informed Johnson of my preference of not having General Grant in the guest box if I decided to kill the president there. To that remark, Johnson assured me he could personally guarantee that General and Mrs. Grant would not be in attendance at the Ford Theater with President Lincoln and his family."

"Why did you insist on not having Mr. and Mrs. Grant present in the box?"

"Because the Grants would have a full contingent of military guards on duty with them and I did not want to face that when entering the box. Simply stated, without the Grants present, I enjoyed far greater odds of carrying out a successful assassination.

"I then pledged my willingness to carry out this supreme act on behalf of the helpless, subjugated Southland whose people I loved and whose cause I gladly championed.

"Johnson then explained that he needed to pull certain strings in his official capacity as vice-president to see that the Grants found themselves elsewhere occupied other than the Ford Theater that evening. He left the room and returned about one hour later donning an evil smile. He extended his hand, and we both shook on the deal. His palm felt cold and clammy to the touch.

"Johnson assured me that the Grants had been called away and that those in attendance with President Lincoln would afford me no interference as I killed him. He also allowed that my escape route would be over the same formerly clandestine thoroughfare over which I had traveled to get to Washington City earlier that day.

"In my escape, I would cross the east end of the Potomac where I had been jailed earlier. The guards at this crossing would be called away, but if any presented themselves to me, I should use the password 'T.B.' or 'T.B. Road.' Johnson assured me any guards present would understand to allow me passage across the river upon hearing these passwords. By then, Johnson explained, he would have been sworn in as president of the United States and would help me in any way possible in my escape and even offer pardon to me if it ever came to that."

I had read about Booth's escape from Washington City and knew that the road he used to get in and out of the city had been the same thoroughfare used by Confederate spies throughout the conflict. I had also read that the route had been discovered by the Yankee government late in the war, a fact limiting its frequent use by Confederates as the fighting came to a close. Toward the end, the route had been under constant watch by troops wearing Yankee blue.

Booth had the choice of a multitude of roads over which to make his escape. The fact that he successfully used the then heavily-guarded Confederate underground route certainly lent credence to the notion of a guiding hand at high levels.

"You possessed a great deal of nerve to agree to use that same route as your escape path, especially since you had been held captive there earlier the same day."

"At first, the thought of using that pathway in my escape caused me much worry and apprehension, and for the very reason you state. Yes, it only made sense that many hundreds of Yankee troops watched the route day and night, and for one very brief moment during my meeting with Johnson, I suspected he might be laying a trap for me. But that thought fled my brain at once when I calculated the degree to which he coveted the presidency of the United States. On more than one occasion during our association, he made statements reflecting his quest for power in general and his intense desire for the office of the presidency in particular. I knew his earnestness in this.

"And so, with my emotions for the southern cause burning deep within me, I regarded the mission before me as a great opportunity to deal the southern people victory out of defeat by slaying Lincoln so as to make way for Andrew Johnson. I deemed him to be a man friendly to the interests of the southern people and who would protect them from tyranny and from the confiscation of their landed estates at the hands of now revengeful abolitionists.

"I left the Kirkwood House and made my way to the Ford Theater. When I reached the alleyway behind the establishment, I spied Loreta Velazquez leaving a nearby residence on what appeared to be personal business. I had met Loreta on more than one occasion while dining at the Kirkwood and knew she belonged to our society. As previously mentioned, she had accompanied me as I surveyed the Ford Theater back when the plan was to kidnap Lincoln. I asked her in what spot along the alleyway would be the choicest spot to tie horses for a man desiring a fast exodus at night. As we surveyed the areas all around the alleyway and she pointed to an area of trees and shrubs.

'That is the best spot. Situate the steeds behind the brush and tie them to one of the lower branches of the trees with brush in front and the animals will not be easily noticed.'"

"When I saw her on my last day in Washington City, we spoke briefly, and I bade her a fond farewell. She was a great friend, but I believe she means much more than that to you. You are a lucky man. Broussard, unlike me, you were smart in your work for the society in not committing a crime so heinous as to mark you for life. I am an assassin who will never know a woman's true love or peace of mind and heart again."

"I have to ask you a question. On that trip to the theater, one of your last to the place, did you tell her of your plan to assassinate the president?"

"No, but a premonition told me she highly suspected that my intentions had grown more sinister. As I think back on it, the combined situation of finding me near the Ford Theater and me telling her she would not see me again probably triggered the forces of her intuition. But enough of that.

"After Loreta departed, I went about the business of preparing for the dastardly deed ahead. I stepped inside the theater and found the box intended for Lincoln, an easy feat since the space had been heavily decorated with patriotic buntings for the evening's grand occasion. I raised the fastenings on the door into the box so that when I entered later that night, no one could open it from the outside afterward.

"I returned to the Kirkwood and loaded the .44-caliber Henry derringer so she would not fail me of fire at the appointed time."

"Did you see Andrew Johnson when you returned?"

"I did. We had drinks at the hotel bar, and I reaffirmed my commitment to carrying out the evil deed previously discussed. We spent a goodly amount of time working out the final details, and Johnson gave me a few new specific instructions necessary for a successful outcome. He told me to make sure of my aim, and I replied I would not fail in my work, that I would shoot the president in the brain. To that, he said, 'Then I am most certainly from now forward the president of the United States.'"

"Do you believe Johnson conspired in this only to become president?"

"No, as much as he craved the office, Johnson was a man who believed that if Lincoln would violate the property rights of the southern people by emancipating slaves, he would also violate their property rights by continuing his policy of the confiscation of their remaining properties.

"We said our adieus and I returned to the theater where I confirmed Lincoln's presence in the decorated box. I hid myself away in a spot selected earlier that day and waited for the appropriate time in the play to make my move.

"When the appointed time arrived, I entered the box stealthily and placed the end of the barrel so close to Lincoln's head that it nearly touched him. Everyone in the box faced away from me entranced by the activities on the stage, a fact making my job all the easier. Wasting no time, I pulled the trigger and fired the shot that inevitably killed the sixteenth president of the United States. In doing so, I propelled to the office the seventeenth president of the United States, Andrew Johnson.

"In almost the same movement that I pulled the trigger, I also jumped from the box and down onto the stage, but not before entangling the spur of my right boot in the decorative drapery on the box. The ensnarement caused me to fall down onto a spot not intended in my plans, a fact that threw my right shinbone against the edge of the stage which fractured it roughly eight inches above the ankle."

Of this specific incident I had read and heard repeated, so I asked him to show me proof.

"Will you show me your leg?"

He rolled up the right leg of his trousers and pointed to an uneven spot on the shinbone that clearly indicated a previous crack in the bone.

To this exhibition, I nodded that I understood its importance.

"Pray, continue."

"I made my exodus from the back of the building and ran as fast as I could on a broken leg to the alleyway and my horse. My associate, David Herold, had held the horse as close as possible to the back entrance as I committed murder inside. To my relief, I found both Herold and the horse waiting in the exact appointed spot when I stepped outside. Herold helped me aboard the horse at once. I kicked the steed with my good leg, and Herold slapped it hard on the rump, acts which sent the beast off into the night toward F Street as if I were riding a winged Pegasus."

"You will pardon me if I ask another question."

"Certainly."

"You say you jumped from the box onto the stage and then immediately made your way to the exit door?"

"That is not exactly true. When I landed upon the stage, I shouted, 'Sic semper tyrannis.' I then ran across the stage and knocked down a one William Withers and took a slash at him with my blade. Then I made for the door."

"Why would you waste precious time in those acts when your life depended on a lightning-fast exit from the building?"

"Because it was important for me to be recognized in order for the conspiracy to succeed."

"Explain that to me."

"Remember when I told you that Johnson and I discussed a few last-minute details before I set out to the Ford Theater? Well, after I killed the president and jumped onto the stage, I then made sure to shout 'Sic semper tyrannis' in part to announce in my own distinct stage voice that I am the actor John Wilkes Booth and in part to allow as many attendees as possible to see my well-publicized face. This was done at the request of Johnson who claimed it as all but necessary for the overall plan to succeed."

"And you trusted him?"

"In this conspiracy I trusted him, but in nothing else. As I said before, there were times when my brain pondered the possibility that Johnson sought to set me up, but the more I considered it, the more I shoved it from my mind completely toward the end. I had to in order to stay focused on my task at hand. Why would Johnson want me apprehended only for me to name him in the conspiracy? Many had witnessed us together over the many months conversing over drinks in the Kirkwood Hotel bar. It served no interest of Johnson for authorities to apprehend me so that I could name him in the conspiracy to kill the president. His plan made all the sense in the world for me to escape completely, not for one night or two but until the end of time, forever tidying up matters and forever easing the mind of the future president.

"Johnson also reminded me of the oath I took when joining the society some years before. I knew he had taken the same oath and that we both stood subject to the authority of the same league, and that he also had to trust the plan to save his own skin just as I had to trust it to save mine.

"But, we digress. Suffice to say, I reached the bridge at the

East Potomac River in a timely manner. A guard stood at the east end of the bridge, and he asked in a clear voice, 'Where are you going?'

"I answered, 'T.B.'

"The guard then asked, 'Where?'

"I answered, 'T.B. Road' as I had been instructed by Johnson.

"The guard then called for help to raise the gate; an act completed forthwith. I then kicked the horse into the same full speed with which we had departed the theater. I made for Surrattville where Herold caught up with me according to plan. We allowed the horses to rest for a few minutes before spending the rest of the night traveling toward the home of Dr. Samuel Mudd."

"Did you know of Dr. Mudd previously, or did you hear about him from someone in Surrattville?"

"I had met Mudd several months before when I purchased a horse from him."

"Did you not feel excruciating pain in your leg?"

"My excitement was such that the pain was somewhat dulled, but definitely forced my pace to be much slower than I liked. Anyway, we reached Dr. Mudd's home around four o'clock in the morning on April 15th. Herold and Mudd helped me off my horse and up the stairs of the Mudd home. Mudd cut off my boot and began an examination of the swollen leg. He then dressed and splint the leg by bandaging it with strips of cloth and carefully cut pieces of cigar boxes. We remained at the Mudd home for the rest of the day and departed as soon as darkness fell with my bootless right foot protected only by Mudd's bandages and pieces of cigar box with a sock covering.

"Around five o'clock in the morning on April 16th, we reached the home of one Mr. Cox, Confederate sympathizer. Cox, having heard of the assassination, refused us admittance, perhaps fearing retribution. However, he did us the kindness of asking his overseer to hide us in a pine thicket near the Potomac River banks behind his plantation.

"I remember the overseer as if I had seen him only yesterday. He stood not quite so tall as myself, but seemed to carry approximately the same weight. His hair and eyes were as black as a raven, and he donned a well-trimmed growth of whiskers over his face. I called him by the name of Johnny, the moniker given many Confederate soldiers. I remember Cox and a Mr. Jones, who I supposed was the half-brother of Cox, calling him Ruddy.

"Ruddy, if that was his actual name, had been a Confederate sympathizer like Cox, his boss, and possessed no moral dilemma whatsoever in delivering us out of harm's way. On our way to the pine thicket, Ruddy told us that some of Colonel Mosby's command of Confederate troops were then stationed south of the Rappahannock River near Bowling Green. Ruddy stated he could deliver us into the safety of these forces for the price of three hundred dollars.

"Of course, we were happy to accept Ruddy's deal. He left us in our hiding place in the pine thicket and proceeded to Bowling Green, a point roughly thirty-six miles distant, to arrange with some of Mosby's men to meet us on the Rappahannock River which then served as the dividing line between the Confederate and Yankee armies still swarming throughout the region."

"Were you not afraid to be left there not knowing when this Ruddy would return?"

"We had no choice. I had also trusted that Johnson would keep any pursuing Yankees off our trail for as long as he possibly could without his devices giving him away. Further, Mr. Jones had accompanied us into the thicket with Ruddy, and he stayed to look after us until Ruddy returned.

"He came back into our camp in the thicket several days later and reported that arrangements had been made with a Captain Jett. Others in Mosby's ranks were to meet us at a ferry near Ports Royal and Conway on the Rappahannock River on April 22nd.

"We began our trek at once, eventually crossing the Potomac to its south side with only eighteen miles left to travel to the agreed upon point on the Rappahannock. The most treacherous leg of our journey lay before us in that region between our position on the Potomac and the endpoint on the Rappahannock. That area was so heavily infested with Yankee soldiers that our discovery could happen at any minute.

"Fearful, terrified in fact, of an easy discovery with my lame leg, I determined to employ a ruse for added protection en route. Near the home of Dr. Stewart, we found an old negro man named Lewis moving across the countryside with a nearly broken-down wagon pulled by two quite depleted and diminished horses. I approached the old man and offered him a handsome price to participate in my journey. He accepted my offer.

"Using wood slats, we made a false bottom in the old man's wagon. We lay straw on the very bottom on which I could lay, and the slats were affixed solidly over me, allowing me just enough space to breathe and move only a little while lying down for the duration of the trip. On the top of the false bottom between the sideboards lay all of the old man's assorted belongings—such items as pots, pans, blankets, mattresses, baskets and farm tools. There were even a few chickens caught up and placed in a split basket fastened securely to the wagon's hind gate.

"So, with roughly eighteen miles left on the journey to the appointed spot on the Rappahannock River, we set out. All along the way, Herold and Ruddy followed along some distance behind so as not to detract from the ruse of an old black man moving from one place to another. Of course, I lay almost motionless and refrained from speaking to old Lewis. In my coat pocket, I carried a few personal belongings, items such as a diary, several checks, a picture of my sister and a few letters. We made the eighteen miles without incident, much to my relief.

"Just as we approached the ferry, old Lewis said he saw soldiers. Just then, I heard a commotion at the back of the wagon, the sound of someone removing everything attached to the hind gate, and then someone grabbed my good foot and pulled me out. I hit the ground on my back and looked up at Herold and Ruddy and silently thanked God they were not Yankee soldiers. With Herold on one side of me and Ruddy on the other, I hobbled as fast as I could onto the ferry where the Confederate soldiers were waiting for us. Those Confederates were the soldiers to which old Lewis referred when he said he saw soldiers . . . not Yankees.

"We got to the other side of the river, and I reached inside my pockets to retrieve money with which to pay Ruddy. In so doing, I discovered that I had lost the assorted belongings I mentioned earlier, those being the picture of my sister, my diary, a handful of letters and even a few extra checks. It dawned on me that the items had come out of my coat pocket because of the hurried manner in which I had been extracted from the wagon. I paid Ruddy and asked him to return to the other side of the river and quickly retrieve my lost articles from the wagon.

"Ruddy replied that he would go back and find the items in the wagon if they were still there and return the articles to me forthwith. The soldiers had arranged to take me to the Garrett home, and Ruddy knew to find me there when he returned with my belongings.

The trio of Ruddy, Herold and Captain Jett stepped into

the boat to go back across the river and then make their way to the wagon. Upon retrieving the items from the wagon, the three had agreed to find me a shoe for my bad foot and other such articles that Herold and I might need on our way across the country.

"In the meantime, I had been introduced to two men connected with Mosby's command, a Lieutenant Ruggles and a Lieutenant Bainbridge whose job it was to escort me to the Garrett home. It was in their company that I swiftly rode away as soon as Ruddy, Herold, and Jett boarded the batteau boat and began making their way back across the water.

"We made it to the Garrett home where Lieutenants Ruggles and Bainbridge left me. They then proceeded to ride off in the distance where they could watch over the Garrett home until such time as Ruddy, Herold, and Jett returned with the items found in the wagon and a shoe for my bad foot. The plan had been for my protective trio to remain near Bowling Green overnight and then return with the goods the very next day.

"So, I spent the night at the Garrett home and awoke the following day highly anticipating the return of the trio carrying the belongings necessary for my continued escape journey. Sometime around two o'clock in the afternoon on April 23rd, Lieutenants Ruggles and Bainbridge rode into the front yard where I lounged and notified me excitedly that I should leave the premises immediately, as a squad of Yankee soldiers had crossed the Rappahannock River in hot pursuit of Lincoln's assassin.

"The two highly suggested I dart at once to a wooded ravine north of the Garrett house and remain there until such time as they returned in roughly one hour's time with a horse for my escape. They advised me to remain as concealed as possible and not to come out until I heard their whistle.

"Naturally, I did as instructed. Without even notifying anyone at the Garrett home, I proceeded hastily to the area north of the house and found an area looking very much like the spot described by Lieutenants Ruggles and Bainbridge. I concealed myself beneath several large clumps of brush and waited for what seemed like an eternity. The pounding of my heart echoed in my brain and beads of sweat poured profusely from my body as I waited nervously.

"Around three or four o'clock I heard the whistle signal and then stepped out of my hiding place in the brush. I was delighted to see my friends with an extra horse in hand. They told me the plan for my escape had changed due to unforeseen obstacles. They no longer believed it prudent for me to wait for the return of my belongings.

The three of us rode off westward at a rapid clip, but not so hurriedly as to wear down our mounts. We kept up a good pace until about midnight when we found a good spot in the woods in which to stop. We were maybe twenty-five miles west of the Garrett home. My two friends conversed with me at length and apprised me of the surrounding countryside while also instructing me as to the exact course for me to take out of the immediate vicinity.

"We shook hands, and I thanked the both of them before offering to pay for their services. They refused to accept my offer of payment and wished me good luck the rest of the way and bade me a fond farewell. We parted ways and, taking their advice, I made my way westward at a good clip for the first solid day before angling off to the southwest on the second.

"They counseled I should masquerade all along the way as a Confederate soldier returning home from the war, and this instruction I took. On the second day out from the Garrett home, I stopped at a farmhouse inhabited by three elderly ladies who took me in as a friendly Confederate. The ladies fed me and my horse and allowed both of us to rest up for as long as needed. I allowed that I should return to my escape trail after only a few hours of resting. I paid the ladies one dollar in silver coin and pushed out.

"Pretending to be a Confederate soldier returning home proved successful for me all along my escape route. Over the course of nearly six days, I continued down through West Virginia and Eastern Kentucky before stopping to rest for nearly a week some fifty or sixty miles southwest of the town of Warfield. There I stayed with a widow lady and her young son while receiving much-needed food, water, and sleep.

"From there, I traveled to the south and found a good spot from which to cross the Mississippi River. My crossing point was at a locale called Catfish Point in the state of Mississippi, a short distance south of where the Arkansas River flows into the Mississippi. After crossing, I set my course for the Indian Territory. Its remoteness of locale deemed it as the best possible hiding place in the world by Lieutenants Ruggles and Bainbridge as well as myself. I had heard of the fighting Confederate Indians of Indian Territory long before and knew that there was no safer place in all the country to hide than with any of those five tribes once fiercely allied with the late Confederacy."

As he spoke, my mind returned to the day I first met St. Helen, or Booth, at General Watie's camp during my last visit to Indian Territory.

"And you must have eventually found your way to General Watie and his fighting Cherokees, for that is where I first met you in his camp after the war had ended."

"You are correct. I enjoyed the protection of the various tribes for approximately eighteen months, and spent considerable time among the Cherokees, before setting out to Nebraska. There in Nebraska City I met a man for whom I worked hauling provisions by wagon train destined for the soldiers stationed at Salt Lake City, Utah. When almost to Salt Lake City, I left the wagon train prematurely without asking for or receiving pay. I set out on my own to San Francisco where I met with my mother and brother, Junius. I remained for a time in California electing to make my way to Mexico where I also spent some considerable time. From there, I eventually found myself in the safe K.G.C. haven of Granbury, Texas where I now reside under the alias, John St. Helen.

"I have now spent many years in the vicinity of Granbury, but plan on inhabiting the environs of Oklahoma Territory very soon. If you are ever in the vicinity of Enid, please find me, as I will be using the alias David E. George."

"There is one last question I have to ask. Did General Watie know that you had recently assassinated the president of the United States?"

"I don't think so. In fact, I highly doubt it. I certainly did not volunteer the information to him. Watie's directive was to keep me concealed and protected for a time and this he did as a loyal member of the society without ever asking me why."

18

THE PROFESSED ASSASSIN
CONTINUES

THE CONVERSATION CONTINUED WITH ME INTERJECTING that I had read many accounts of the assassination in which the government of the United States positively claimed that John Wilkes Booth had been shot dead in the Garrett Barn. Furthermore, I told him I had read that his body had been speedily returned to Washington City and brought aboard the Montauk, the ironclad sea vessel, and then promptly buried in Washington City's old penitentiary, then being used as an arsenal. A supposed handful of officials were given the opportunity to inspect the body before its descent six feet under.

"Broussard, I hope the entire world believes that official story of the government of the United States, at least long enough for me to live a while longer. But, from one K.G.C. agent to another, I will do you the honor of presenting a few observations that I would not lay before anyone else, and you can arrive at your own conclusions.

"But before I lay before you the reasons that I am John Wilkes Booth, I want to thank you for hearing my story.

Whether you believe my story as told by John St. Helen, an imposter, or by John Wilkes Booth the known murderer, matters not as much to me as you might think. You have done me a great kindness in hearing me recount what I needed to desperately relate to another human being. I have told you my story in good faith and have misled you in no way whatsoever, so, Drouet Broussard, I thank you for allowing me to unburden my heart and soul.

"Now, I know that after tonight I shall never see you again, so what follows is told in the same good faith as everything else recounted up to this point. From now on, you will wonder about the legitimacy of my story. What evidence have I to lend it support, you may ponder, before we go our separate ways? I give you my answer in five parts.

"First, you have to wonder how it was that I escaped through what everyone acknowledges were the nearly impenetrable federal lines after assassinating President Lincoln. I was in no way associated with anyone in the federal army to gain access across the bridge on that dark night. The only way this could be accomplished was through the intervention and authority of high-ranking Vice-President Johnson.

"Secondly, how was it that David Herold, one of my chief co-conspirators, also passed over the same point on the same bridge by the same guard and was then able to catch up with me at Surrattville?

"Third, under no circumstances would I have entered Lincoln's box at the theatre without the assurance that Grant and his wife would not be in attendance with the president. The newspapers had reported the Grants' upcoming presence with Lincoln that night, and yet, he was somehow called away from Washington City to attend to matters elsewhere. Again, this could not have been accomplished without the assistance of Andrew Johnson, a partner in the conspiracy.

"Fourth, don't you find it interesting that the body was so hastily placed in the ground barely two days after retrieving it from the Garrett barn? They have the body of one of the most wanted assassins in the history of the world, and they do not keep it topside long enough to allow only but a few men to identify the body. Why? I can tell you why. Because John Wilkes Booth sits before you now and someone else was shot in Garrett's barn, and their body brought back to Washington City and buried at breakneck speed in the ground at the old penitentiary as a part of the concealment conspiracy.

"And, fifth, don't you find it interesting that I sit before you now to collect information and financial resources from you, an agent of the K.G.C., for duties performed? Were I not the man who assassinated the president of the United States, then, pray, why do you sit before me holding an envelope packed tightly with contents meant for me? The society to which we belong does not spend good money after bad, that much I can tell you. Those in the upper echelons of our cabal know exactly what I did to earn the contents of the envelope you now hold. They pay me to keep quiet about an assassination that changed history. They would have me killed for mentioning any of this, even to you.

"That is all I can tell you from where I sit at this point in time, but I can assure you that more information will be uncovered in years to come to bear out my story."

"Do you have any regrets for your actions?"

"Every day I live with regret. I now believe that the man I killed was one of the greatest men to ever live, a man who did what he thought was right, who maintained the union of the United States and who did not sell out the country to foreign interests to do it.

"And I live with regret over the death of another."

"Who might that be?"

"Mary Surratt. Mary Surratt was hung by her neck for a crime in which she played no part whatsoever. No day passes that I do not think of that good and noble and beautiful woman who met her dark end because of my actions.

"Broussard, do you ever look long and hard at photographs? Do you ever look deep into a photograph at the people going to and fro around the central subject, at people years before who went along unaware that they are stared at by the future? That point in time did not last but for only a few seconds; yet, that moment lives on, and it spreads across the ages when we see it today. Like so many moments in photographs, I wish my words about Mary Surratt could carry across time like that to all of the civilized people here today and to those yet to be born."

"What about Ruddy, the man killed at the Garrett barn?"

"Not a day goes by that I don't think about the possibility that the man I knew as Ruddy unintentionally gave his life for mine. That is why I carry with clarity the memory of his looks and demeanor. If the man they killed was, in fact, Ruddy then, yes, I feel great sorrow and allow that I should never have entered Lincoln's box at the theater and killed him on that fateful night."

The time came for me to escort my friend back to his room near Camp and First Streets. We departed the club, boarded the carriage and made our way back using the same devious route as before, going along in an unassuming fashion and blending in with the darkness and shadows of buildings.

Before stepping down off the carriage to begin his walk to the side door of the residence, my friend and I exchanged heart-felt words of good luck and good fortune to one another, both of us expressing that the drink and conversation had ended all too soon. We shook hands, he stepped down and began walking to his room, but turned back to me with one last remark.

"I saw the way you looked at me tonight at the club. I saw in your countenance that you beheld not only me. I know you also saw the shadow people who walk with me."

I did not answer but merely tipped my hat toward him as the carriage pulled away.

19

LIFE AND DEATH GOES ON

IN THE DAYS AND WEEKS AFTER THE PROFESSED ASSASSIN departed New Orleans, Loreta and I discussed the conspiracy in which he claimed his noteworthy role.

As it turns out, Loreta had known of the early meetings in New Orleans between Booth, Pike, Slidell, and Benjamin in which they planned for the assassination of Abraham Lincoln. She had known those plans were abandoned for a time as Booth and his group in Washington City concocted a plan to kidnap the president so as to use him to free Confederate prisoners during the war. She claimed ignorance of Booth's plan to assassinate the president after the surrender at Appomattox and stated that her brief encounter with Booth near the Ford Theater on the day of the assassination had been a mere coincidence.

Loreta had also known of the planned visit of John St. Helen to New Orleans for the sole purpose of meeting with me. I had heard her mention the name at the Comus ball and fathomed then that she enjoyed a larger K.G.C. network of contacts than did I.

I asked Loreta why she never mentioned John Wilkes Booth before. She answered that she did not want to risk losing my admiration over the association. She then asked me why I never broached the subject with her, and I answered that I did not want to risk losing her affection by insinuating a connection with the assassin.

It seemed we both possessed enough wisdom to let sleeping dogs lie undisturbed.

Through our mutual K.G.C. contacts, but mainly through hers, as well as from newspaper reports and other sources, we were able to ascertain certain other facts concerning the assassination over the subsequent months and years.

We learned that when David Herold ran out of Garrett's barn, he shouted to Luther Baker and the rest of the party that the man he left behind inside was not John Wilkes Booth. One would have to believe Sergeant Corbett shot the man in the barn believing him Lincoln's assassination.

We learned of Joseph Zisgen and Wilson D. Kenzie, Yankee soldiers present with Luther Baker and the rest of the party at Garrett's barn. They recounted a much different narrative than the version given by the Baker brothers who likely coordinated their story which became the official version of the United States government. Zisgen and Kenzie both stated that the corpse turned over to Lafayette Baker did not feature a broken leg. We speculated the brothers Baker had the corpse's leg broken while en route to Washington City to make the body look like that of Booth so they could claim their share of the reward money.

Sources told us that both Zisgen and Kenzie later dropped out of sight and kept their account to themselves after none other than Lafayette Baker threatened them with their lives.

Also, Dr. John Frederick May, summoned to the Yankee ship Montauk, on which the corpse had been taken by Luther

Baker and company immediately upon arriving in Washington City, stated in no uncertain terms that the corpse did not resemble John Wilkes Booth. "There is no resemblance in that corpse to Booth, nor can I believe it to be him."

We also received reports that roughly eighteen pages of Booth's diary were missing when the journal was removed from a war department file in Washington City a few years after the assassination. The diary had never been used in the 1865 conspiracy trial. Loreta strongly believed the missing pages incriminated Lafayette Baker and that her former boss in the National Detective Bureau had them extracted to hide his own involvement in the affair.

Loreta, familiar with the Yankee chain of command in Washington City at the time, said the search for Booth *should* have been orchestrated by General Christopher Augur, then in command of the Twenty-Second Army Corps and the military district of Washington City. She told me in the strongest terms that Augur should have been in charge of the capture, death, identification, and burial of the assassin but knew on good authority that he never had been notified. She believed Augur had been intentionally cut out so that Lafayette Baker, reporting to the secretary of war Stanton, could orchestrate the ruse and collect the reward money.

The firestorm of protest over the matter in Washington City at the time reinforced her belief.

Senator Garrett Davis of Kentucky said he never saw any satisfactory evidence that Booth was killed. He went on to say, "I would rather have better testimony of the fact. I want proof that Booth was in that barn. I cannot conceive if he was in that barn, why he was not taken alive as was ordered. I have not seen anybody, or any evidence of anybody, that identified Booth after he was said to be killed. Why so much secrecy about it? Booth could have been captured just as well alive or dead. It would have been more satisfactory to have him brought here alive and to have inquired of him to reveal the whole transaction. Or bring his body up here, let all who have seen him playing, all who had associated with him on stage, tavern, and other public places have access to his body to have identified it."

Davis' remarks, which had been aimed at the secretary of war Stanton, represented many people in Washington City and around the country at the time who believed the Yankee cabinet member had much to conceal in the matter. Loreta told me Stanton and Baker had been a formidable team, with her former boss serving as the strong-arm thug of the partnership while often taking direct orders from Stanton, the mastermind.

Nevertheless, Loreta and I put the matter out of our minds and went about living our lives together. We had given much of our time and energies to the K.G.C. and were purposeful in moving forward to new endeavors. We were wise enough to know that many of our questions might never be answered.

Some years later, however, around 1903, I strode into the Pickwick Club, and someone handed me a newspaper from Enid, Oklahoma Territory along with an envelope. The pages of the paper had already been turned to a page showcasing the following story: "Booth" Dies, Enid Man Claimed to be Lincoln's Assassin, Crowds Throng Funeral Parlor, Identification Sought."

According to the story, a man claiming the identity of John Wilkes Booth passed away at the Grand Avenue Hotel in Enid, Oklahoma Territory. He went by the name David George. In his deathbed confession, he said he wanted to unburden his soul of guilt over the hanging of Mary Surratt and wanted to clear her name. He had been a resident of Enid for several years and lived a solitary life with no friends or family known to anyone in Enid. Large crowds thronged to the funeral parlor where his body lay inside.

Crowds gathered outside the Kaufman funeral parlor in Enid when news of the man's death was released. Some in the crowd demanded that the body be handed over to a lynch mob.

Loreta and I later learned that the mysterious resident of the Grand Avenue Hotel in Enid had arrived there fresh out of the state of Texas where, the story claimed, he had dishonored a young lady whose affections he won through less than gentlemanly devices. Once in the territory, he claimed to be a house painter by profession but no one ever saw him paint a house, and yet he never fell short of money. He sometimes performed in the local plays in Enid and always mesmerized the audiences with his riveting portrayals. Before making his home in Enid, he resided for a time in El Reno, Oklahoma Territory and, before that, in Guthrie, the Oklahoma Territorial capital. In both of those cities, he had performed in the local plays and brought down the house each time with his performances. Everywhere he went, locals sensed he did not belong among them and wondered among themselves as to his true identity and background.

The Kaufman funeral parlor in Enid had infused the assassin's corpse with so much arsenic that it became an almost mummified display in Pennaman's Furniture Store adjacent to the funeral parlor. The corpse stayed in the front window in hopes that its former owner could be identified and funeral costs obtained.

After reading the newspaper story, I opened the envelope and from within extracted a photograph which I inspected closely. I own the very photograph to this day, and its subject is none other than the man I met in New Orleans and to whom I handed checks and other material from the K.G.C., John St. Helen, also known as David George, and who I know beyond a shadow of a doubt to have been none other than John Wilkes Booth. The photograph featured the professed assassin's corpse sitting in a chair in the window of the aforementioned Pennaman's Furniture Store in Enid.

It turns out a lawyer identified the body, paid the funeral costs and took it back to his Memphis, Tennessee home where he displayed it. The following year, in 1904, the lawyer had the body displayed at the St. Louis World's Fair as the body of John Wilkes Booth. The lawyer continued displaying the body in his home until such time as he died and his widow sold the artifact to a traveling carnival.

The shadow people had seemingly escorted the actor and assassin to a highly fantastic and grotesque final act. His earthly deeds had sadly designated him to further degradation after passing through the veil of this life.

As for Loreta and me, we made New Orleans our home. Marguerite, father's mistress, along with certain members of her family, had lived in father's home after it became safe to stay there. I eventually deeded the property to her, as I felt Father would have wanted this, too. I kept the apartment in the Vieux Carre and Loreta, and I divided our time in New Orleans between it and her home on Prytania Street.

Loreta had traveled throughout the west before we met and told many stories describing the rugged grandeur found in the mountains and deserts of places like Colorado, New Mexico, and California. We traveled to those places many times but always returned to the New Orleans with great joy and anticipation of the sights and sounds of our beloved city.

We lived mainly in the Vieux Carre apartment. We frequented the old haunts there as well as the new, always enjoying the spirit of fun and frolic as much a part of the area as the bricks and mortar of its ancient buildings along its streets and alleyways.

We enjoyed the new sounds as well as the old. We heard the music of Emile "Whiskey" Benrod, Willie "Cajun" Bussey, Frank "Monk" Bussey, "Slew-foot" Pete and a fellow named "Warm Gravy." This group of young street urchins whose musical instruments were cigar box guitars, cheese box banjos, washboards, kettles, cowbells, gourds filled with pebbles and stovepipes emerged. They called themselves the Razzy Dazzy Spasm Band, and they specialized in fast tempos and chord-based improvisation. Some say they were the first jazz band. We stood mesmerized hearing former slaves strumming the guitars and singing the beautiful sing-song poetry of suffering. Seemingly, many had been given the chance for new beginnings with their vocalized artistry.

We came to terms with our past life together, fighting and working on behalf of the Confederacy and that certain society that worked toward a goal that we both deemed dubious in hindsight. However, along with others of the time, we believed in our cause, and neither of us ever apologized for our work on behalf of Southern independence.

One evening in the apartment, as the wine and Sazerac flowed freely, we discussed how much remained of father's estate and the mint heist loot. I explained that some of the mint building take had been used toward paying certain K.G.C. operatives, but that enough remained from it and father's estate to provide an adequate income for the both of us for many years.

"Adequate won't do, Drouet. Not for us. We will always want and do more than what is considered *adequate*."

"What do you mean?"

"I mean that even though the Yankees succeeded in defeating the Confederacy, they never defeated you and me. We hoodwinked them at every turn and never once did they find us out, at least not in time to do anything about it. We slid through the fingertips of history,"

I nodded that I understood her meaning. The game would always be afoot for her and me in some form or fashion.

Then, she reached into a satchel and extracted three electrotype plates used to counterfeit Yankee notes and bonds during the war, the same type of plates she had described to me before when recounting her exploits as a double agent in the United States Treasury.

"Drouet, I still know certain people who can make these work for you and me. What say you?"

Smiling, I gave her a crisp salute with my hand.

"I hope you know I love you, Drouet Broussard."

Taking her by the hand, I drew her to me and inhaled her sweet scent.

"Madame, I return you affections ten-fold and will forever be your loving co-conspirator."

I never could predict that woman.

Finis

Ghost Knights Of New Orleans
ISBN: 978-4-86747-400-6

Published by
Next Chapter
1-60-20 Minami-Otsuka
170-0005 Toshima-Ku, Tokyo
+818035793528

18th May 2021

Lightning Source UK Ltd.
Milton Keynes UK
UKHW012058030621
384904UK00001B/204